TROUBLE IN
THE VALLEY

ROBERT VAUGHAN

WOLFPACK
PUBLISHING
— EST 2013 —

WOLFPACK
PUBLISHING
— EST 2013 —

Trouble In The Valley
Paperback Edition
Copyright © 2021 Robert Vaughan

Wolfpack Publishing
6032 Wheat Penny Avenue
Las Vegas, NV 89122

Paperback ISBN: 978-1-64734-345-3
Ebook ISBN: 978-1-64734-856-4

TROUBLE IN THE VALLEY

CHAPTER ONE

Patrick Flannigan waited in the boardroom of the Thrift Savings and Loan of Denver. At the moment, he was the only one in the boardroom, and he sat at the long, highly polished table, drumming his fingers on the folder that lay before him. The folder contained all the economic files pertaining to the Valley Spur, a short line that ran from Boise, Idaho, to Jordan Valley, Oregon.

Pat had been an employee of the railroad for five years, starting as a construction chief, supervising the laying of the track. He had taken a reduction in pay in lieu of Valley Spur Railroad stock. Initially he had been given two-hundred-fifty shares, and subsequently he had managed to buy an additional one-hundred-one shares, to give him three-hundred fifty-one shares of the two-thousand shares outstanding. The stock, which had initially been valued at one-hundred dollars a share, was now worth twenty-five dollars a share. As a result of the railroad's continual loss of revenue, Pat had been informed that the railroad was about to stop operation.

The meeting this morning was to formalize the close, but Pat had other ideas, and his ideas were backed up by the documents he had in the folder.

E.T. Cummins, owned five hundred shares and was, by virtue of being the largest share-holder, the president of the Valley Spur Railroad. He was the one who had notified Pat of his plans to shut down the railroad.

Cummins arrived with the other two major stockholders, and the three men took their seat around the table.

"Ah, Mr. Flannigan, you are here early I see," Cummins said by way of greeting. "Good, good, one thousand shares of stock are herein present, so I am calling the meeting to order."

"Gentlemen, it cannot come as a shock to you to hear that the hopes we had for the Valley Spur Railroad have not borne fruit. The line has steadily lost money, and now our operating capital has been exhausted. As I said in my post to each of you, I see no option, other than shutting the railroad down. We could try and sell our rolling stock, but I doubt there would actually be a market for it."

"Well, Abe, what do you think we should do with it?" Lucas Parish asked.

"Hell, we don't need to do anything with it. Just leave it parked until it turns to rust, as far as I'm concerned."

"I don't think we should shut down," Pat said.

"You have no problem with letting the railroad just continue to bleed money?" Cummins asked.

"Don't be crazy, Flannigan, we have no choice. We must shut down."

"There's an alternative," Pat suggested.

"And what would that be?" Cummins asked.

"I will buy you three out, at one dollar a share."

"One dollar? Are you kidding? This stock was issued at one hundred dollars a share," Cunningham said.

"And what is its value now?" Pat asked.

"What do you mean? I know it's not worth a hundred dollars a share now, but it has to be worth more than a dollar a share."

"Really? A moment ago, you were willing to just shut down. How much is stock for a non-existent railroad worth?"

"Nothing," Parish said. "I think he's got us there, Abe."

"We are talking cash, are we not, Flannigan?" Cunningham asked. "No options or any kind of gimmick."

"I am prepared to present each of you with a draft that you can cash at this very bank" Pat said.

"When will we get the money?" Cunningham asked.

Pat opened the file. "Mr. Cunningham, you hold one hundred shares. I have a draft on this bank for one-hundred dollars made out to you. Mr. Parish, you hold one-hundred-fifty shares, and I have a check for you for that amount, and Mr. Cummins, I have five-hundred dollars for you."

"All right give me the money," Cunningham said.

Pat shook his head, then pulled out three more sheets of paper. "Before I give you the money, I want you to sign these documents, transferring your shares to me."

"How do we know these checks are worth anything?" Parish asked.

Pat held up a finger, as if telling them to wait for one moment, then stepped to the door, and called out.

"Mr. Schulenberg, would you please step in here?"

Dwight Schulenberg, who was president of the Thrift Savings and Loan of Denver, stepped into the room.

"How may I help you, Mr. Flannigan?" he asked with a smile on his face.

"My associates want to know if these checks are any good," Pat replied.

"Oh, yes indeed," Schulenberg said, assuring the others. "You may present them to any teller and redeem them for cash."

"Mr. Schulenberg, did you bring your notary seal with you?"

"I did."

"I would like for you to notarize these documents for me, as each of them is signed."

The three men signed the documents, Pat presented the checks, and with that action he was now the majority owner of the Valley Spur Railroad line.

So, he asked himself, what next?

* * *

It was perhaps because Sterling Cassidy was possessed of a great respect for education that he had allowed his daughter, Nora, to take part in a unique experiment. Nora had returned to the east to study at Swansdale University, where Cassidy himself had once taught. For some time, the only field of study open to women had been Liberal Arts, but now women were being accepted in more vocationally oriented curriculums, so Sterling had sent Nora to the university to study math and accounting.

Sterling had kissed Nora goodbye, telling her how proud he would be when she returned with her degree in hand. Now she was returning home having completed her studies.

Nora shifted in her seat, trying for the thousandth time to find some way to get comfortable. It was impossible. Though she had been on the train for only five days, she felt as if her journey had no beginning and would have no end. It seemed she had always been on the train, and she could scarcely remember a time when her legs weren't cramped, and her bottom didn't hurt. She was dirty from smoke and soot and hot and sticky from five days without a bath.

The train began slowing, and Nora looked out the window. A handful of small, weather-beaten buildings slid by, then there was a station platform, and finally a depot. There were half a dozen horses and as many buckboards around the depot. It was just one of the many typical trackside towns along the western reaches of the railroad. Nora knew there would be many more before she reached Jordan Valley, Oregon, where her father published the *Jordan Valley Monitor*, a weekly newspaper.

"Ma'am, this here is Twin Falls," the conductor said. "You'll be wantin' to get off here, if you're goin' on to Oregon."

"Thank you," Nora said. She stood up as the train squealed to a stop, then walked stiffly on legs sore from days of sitting. When she stepped down from the train her one piece of baggage was already on the platform, colorful now with the destination tags of the several railroads she had thus far ridden.

Nora walked into the small, wooden depot building. A potbellied stove sat in the middle of the room, and though there was no fire now, it was black from the soot of long use. There was a wooden bench near the stove, and a highly polished brass spittoon near the bench. Despite the spittoon, a cigar had been thoughtlessly ground out on the wide plank boards of the floor.

The wall of the depot sported a calendar, with all the days crossed off until today's date: June 15, 1881. The picture on the calendar was of a night train crossing a trestle between two pine tree-covered mountains. The train's headlight speared forward in the darkness, and the tiny windows of the cars glowed golden. Nora laughed at the romanticized painting. The cars would be dark inside, she knew, and the people would be trying to sleep. Unsuccessfully, she added, with the experience of four such nights behind her.

Beside the calendar a clock ticked loudly, and beside the clock there was a printed time schedule. There were two ticket sales windows, but they were both closed. Despite the activity on the platform outside, the depot was empty, so Nora sat on the bench to wait.

Nora heard the conductor call, "All aboard," then the rush of steam and the clatter of slack being jerked out of the cars as the train started. She looked through the window and watched the train leave. Only after it was gone, did the stationmaster come in. He looked surprised to see her sitting there.

"Something I can do for you, ma'am?" the stationmaster asked.

"Yes," Nora said. "I'd like a ticket to Jordan Valley, Oregon, please." Nora began to open her purse.

"Ma'am, they isn't anything I can do about that," he said. "The fact is, they aren't any trains going to Jordan Valley."

"What?" Nora asked, surprised. "But I don't understand. The Valley Spur line tracks pass right through Jordan Valley."

"Yes ma'am, the tracks pass through Jordan Valley, but unfortunately, the trains don't."

"Of course, they do. I rode a train the last time I left home, and that was less than a year ago."

"Quite a bit has happened, just in the last six months, ma'am, most of it bad. The Valley Spur line fell on hard times. They only have one train, and it isn't running anymore."

"But...what about the railroad I was just on?" Nora asked. "Couldn't they run one of their trains on the Valley Spur line tracks?"

The stationmaster laughed. "No, ma'am, the tracks don't belong to them, so they couldn't use them, and like as not they wouldn't do such a thing for one passenger, even if they could."

"Maybe they'd make an exception for someone as pretty as this young lady," a new voice said.

Nora turned toward the sound of the voice. It was a man, tall, rawboned, and with a thick head of sandy hair. He had an easy, engaging smile. The man bowed slightly, not stiffly or formally, but gracefully.

"I'm Patrick Flannigan, ma'am," the tall stranger said. "I'm with the Valley Spur line. Is there something I can do for you?"

"I must get to Jordan Valley," Nora said. "I know the Valley Spur line trains used to go through there. When did they stop? And why did they stop?"

"They stopped about three months ago," Pat said. "And as to the why, they stopped when the cost of operation became greater than the gross income. Of course, I don't want to bore someone as pretty as you with the details of the business. You aren't supposed to understand such things."

"Mr. Flannigan, I have had four years of business and accounting, as well as corporation law at Swansdale University. I can read a profit and loss statement as well as anyone."

Pat Flannigan smiled at Nora's haughty reply. "I'm sorry," he said easily. "I didn't mean to imply that you were not smart enough or anything. It's just that women don't normally…"

Now it was Nora's turn to smile and apologize.

"Please forgive me," she said. "It's just that I have had to deal with this same sort of thing for the last four years, and I'm somewhat defensive about being a woman."

"Miss, if you ask me, you have nothing at all to be defensive about." Pat rubbed his chin with his hand and studied Nora for a moment.

"Perhaps I am too hasty," Nora finally managed to mumble.

"Did you say you wanted to go to Jordan Valley?"

"Yes."

"I might be able to help you."

"You can get me to Jordan Valley?"

"I can't get you to Jordan Valley, but I can get you to Boise. From there you can get to Jordan Valley by stage," Pat said.

"How?" Nora asked. "I mean, what do you have in mind?"

"I have to take an engine to Boise. You could go with me if you don't mind riding in the engine cab."

"Ride in the engine cab?" Nora asked. "Why, I wouldn't know what to do."

Pat laughed. "You wouldn't have to do anything at all," he said. "I'd do all the work. I even have to fire the boiler myself, because right now I don't have the money to hire a crew, so there won't be a fireman."

"Flannigan, you can't let a passenger ride in the engine cab," the stationmaster said. "It's against company policy."

Pat laughed. "You forget, Eb, that I am the company now, so I make the rules. And the rules are that if a beautiful young woman in distress needs a ride to Boise, she can ride in the engine cab with me. Now, how about it, miss, what do you say? Do you want to come along?"

All the commonsense Nora could muster screamed at her to say no! How could she possibly think of going on such a journey with a strange man? And yet, the thrill and excitement of riding in the cab of a locomotive was stronger than the warning voices that shouted in her mind. Besides, there was some justification to accepting the offer. She did need to get home, and this appeared to be the only way.

Nora smiled at Pat.

"Yes," she said, "I accept your kind offer."

CHAPTER TWO

Pat grabbed Nora's suitcase and started across the tracks to a side-track, where a single, steam-blowing engine sat waiting.

"I've already fired her up," he said, "so we can get going right away."

As Nora approached the big engine, the thought of what she was doing began to sink in. As it sank in, it became more frightening to her.

"I know it's supposed to be ladies first," Pat said. "But you'd better let me climb up first, then I'll help you."

"All right," Nora said. She was standing by the wheels, marveling at the size and power of the locomotive. The wheels were taller than she was, and she had to look up to see the top of the rim. The wheel rims were white; the engine itself was green, with red and brass trim.

Pat saw her looking at the engine, and he paused for just a moment before he climbed up.

"Isn't she beautiful?"

"I beg your pardon?"

"The engine," Pat said. "She was the most beautiful engine we had on the line. I'm glad I was able to save it."

"Yes," Nora said. She hadn't really looked at it in that way, but there was a sense of beauty in all the awesome power the engine showed.

Pat climbed into the cab, then stretched his hand down toward Nora's. "All aboard for the...what's your name, miss?"

"Nora Cassidy."

"All aboard for the Nora Cassidy Special."

Nora took Pat's hand

Inside the engine, there was a maze of pipes, valves, switches, and gauges. There was a small, cushioned seat on one side of the engine cab, and an iron seat, like the seat of a bicycle, on the other side. Pat moved to the bicycle seat and began twisting a valve, as if turning on water.

"Have a seat," he invited generously, pointing to the cushioned bench.

Nora sat down gratefully and watched as Pat twisted the valves. There were so many that she had no idea how anyone would know where to start.

"Are you an engineer?" she asked.

"Yes," Pat said. He turned a valve, and there was a sudden puff of steam. Pat jumped, then started twisting it frantically, until the steam stopped.

"Wrong valve," he said sheepishly.

"Haven't you ever driven this engine before?" Nora asked.

"Nope," Pat replied easily. He twisted another valve, and this time the steam was vented into the right place. The train began to roll. "Ah, that's the one I need," he said. He looked at Nora and smiled proudly, and to Nora, he had the look of a little boy who had just done something right.

"Isn't it amazing," she said, "that turning that one valve could make this big engine move?"

"Yes, isn't it?"

"Which valve stops it?" Nora asked.

"Which valve stops it?" Pat replied, looking puzzled by the question. "You know, that's a good question. I guess we really should know that, shouldn't we? I mean in case we want to stop."

Nora laughed nervously. "You are teasing, aren't you?"

"No, I'm quite serious," Pat said. "We really should know how to stop this thing. I mean, what if we had to apply the brakes suddenly? Wouldn't it be to our advantage to know how to do it?"

"What are you talking about?" Nora asked, now more nervous than before.

"Look around, will you? It's probably shaped like a long lever, or handle, or something."

By now the train was rolling along at a pretty good clip, and Nora was becoming quite apprehensive about the whole thing. Had she placed her life in the hands of an incompetent?

"Why are you asking me?" she asked. "Where is the brake on the other engines? Aren't they pretty much alike?"

"I don't know," Pat admitted. "This is the only engine I've ever driven."

"What? I thought you said you'd never driven *this* engine."

"I haven't," Pat said. "Until right now."

"You mean you've never driven *any* engine before this?" Nora gasped.

"Nope," Pat said.

"But…but you said you were an engineer?"

"I am."

"An engineer who has never driven a train?"

"Oh," Pat said easily. "Did you mean *that* kind of an engineer? Oh, no, I'm not a train engineer, I'm a construction engineer. I built this railroad."

"A construction engineer?" Nora asked in a weak voice.

"Ah," Pat said, putting his hand on a lever and smiling broadly in pride of accomplishment. "Here it is. Were all set now."

"Oh," Nora said. She had a hollow feeling in the pit of her stomach. She was with a madman. "We are going to be killed."

"No, we'll be all right," Pat insisted. He laughed. "One thing for sure, we can't get lost, can we? What's there to driving this thing? All I have to do is follow the tracks."

"You're crazy," Nora said.

"I'm crazy?" Pat said. "I didn't trust *my* life to someone who had never driven one of these things before."

Nora looked at Pat as if he were raving. Then suddenly the outrageously bizarre humor of the situation struck her, and she began to laugh. She laughed so long and so hard that tears came to her eyes, and her side hurt, and she had to hold her arms across her stomach.

Pat laughed with her, and he jerked on the whistle cord, so that the very engine seemed to join in.

"You're quite a girl, Nora Cassidy," he finally said, wiping his own eyes with his finger. "And 'tis proud I am to be havin' your company on this trip."

"'Tis proud I am to be along," Nora said, giving a good impression of Pat's Irish brogue.

Pat worked hard at keeping the fire stocked, throwing chunks of wood into blazing flames in the firebox. He kept the throttle open all the way, and though Nora had no way of knowing, they were running nearly sixty miles an hour. She did realize that it was much faster than any of the trains she had been on before. A few times she grew brave enough to stick her head out the window, peering ahead along the long, gracefully curved boiler, letting the wind blow through her hair and force her eyes into narrow slits. It was fascinating, watching the twin rails, so slender in the distance that they seemed to touch, yet opening wider and wider until they seemed to pass to either side of them as they raced by. The engine pounded across a bridge, and she could hear the thunder of their crossing. Then the track swept around a sharp curve, hemmed in by rocky bluffs to either side.

When the train came out of the narrow gorge, the valley opened up wide, with grassy fields, sparkling water, and large, beautiful trees. Pat began twisting valves, and finally he pulled the brake lever, to bring the engine to a halt.

"What are we doing?" Nora asked. "Why did you stop?"

"Raise the cushion, and look inside," Pat ordered.

Nora opened the cushion and saw that the bench she had been sitting on was actually a storage chest. Inside the chest, she saw a picnic basket

"A picnic basket?"

"We have to eat something," Pat said. "And I didn't bother to attach a dining car. Come on, there's a nice place over there, by the water." Pat took the basket and started to climb down.

"Is it safe to leave the train here?" Nora asked.

Pat laughed. "No one is going to come along and hit it," he said. "This is the only engine on the line."

"Yes, but no better than you are at operating it, who's to say the engine won't run away and leave us stranded?"

"Touché, my girl, touché," Pat replied, laughing. "But I'm pretty sure we'll be all right."

Pat helped Nora down, then he walked to the rear of the wood tender and reached down inside a burlap bag.

"What's that?" Nora asked.

"It's a trick I learned," Pat said. "You soak a burlap bag in water, then hang it out and let the wind blow across it. As the wind causes the water to evaporate, it cools...ah, here it is," Pat pulled out a bottle of wine. "It cools the wine. Feel this. It's just as cold as if it had been buried in a snowbank."

Nora felt the bottle and was amazed at how cold it really was.

"What do we have for lunch?" Nora asked.

"Are you hungry?"

"Yes."

Pat laughed. "Good. I like a woman who isn't afraid to admit that she has an appetite for food. An appetite for food means you also have an appetite for life." Pat looked inside. "I don't know what we have, really. I paid Mrs. Minerva at the boardinghouse to prepare a picnic lunch for me."

"Oh, I wouldn't want to take any of your lunch," Nora said. "If she prepared for only one..."

Pat laughed again. "You don't understand how Mrs. Minerva does things," he said. "She was married for forty years to Big Ernest, who weighed about 300 pounds, and stood about six feet seven. She thinks every man eats the way Big Ernest used to eat, so she fixes the lunches accordingly. Then, God forbid you shouldn't get hungry later, so she puts enough in for a snack."

This time it was Nora's turn to laugh. "Is Big Ernest still around?"

"No, he died about five years ago. Mrs. Minerva is sure it was because he was hungry. I just hope it wasn't acute indigestion. Ah, we have cold chicken and roast beef, potato salad, sliced cucumbers, baked bread, and a whole cake."

Pat found a flat rock and spread out the red and white checkered tablecloth which Mrs. Minerva had folded in the basket, then set out the food. There were two cups in the basket, and these he filled with wine. He gave a cup to Nora.

"Thank you," Nora said. "Oh, everything looks so good," she said. She took a swallow of wine and looked out across the valley. The field before them waved with flowers of every hue and description. There were the white and yellow oxeye daisies, the slender white and blue columbines, and the brilliant red Indian paintbrushes. Beyond the valley, a great range of snow-capped mountains rose.

"I had almost forgotten how beautiful our part of the country is," she said.

"Are you just coming back from school?" Pat asked.

"Yes," Nora said. "I hope Papa will be happy to see me."

"I'm certain he will," Pat said. "Were you born out here?"

"No, I was born in Baltimore. My father was a college professor there, but it had long been his ambition to go west and begin a newspaper, so, when I was ten years old, he did just that. He now publishes the *Jordan Valley Monitor*."

"I've heard of the paper," Pat said. "It enjoys an excellent reputation."

"How nice of you to say so," Nora said.

"I'm merely speaking the truth," Pat said. "I'm from the east, too, by the way. I'm from Boston."

"Boston is a lovely city," Nora said. "My father has many colleagues in the universities there."

Pat laughed, self-deprecatingly. "I'm sure your father's colleagues and my family never crossed paths. My father was a policeman, Irish born, and my mother a charwoman. Sure 'n 'twas to escape such a life that I left the city as a boy of sixteen, lured by promises of adventure and glory in 'Custer's Own'."

"Custer's Own?"

"The Seventh Cavalry," Pat said. "'Twas a fine military organization, composed in the main of Irishmen like myself." Pat rolled his r's, and Nora laughed.

"Sometimes you have a terrible brogue, and sometimes you have none. I never know if you are putting on an act or not."

"Sure, 'n you've discovered my secret, darlin'," Pat said. "For the truth is, I learned long ago that a brogue was not always the best thing to have, so I worked at discarding it. I can still use it if it comes in handy, such as working with a hard-headed bunch of Irish gandy dancers."

"What's a gandy dancer?"

Pat discarded the chicken bone, then made himself a thick roast beef sandwich before he went on.

"A gandy dancer is a railroad worker," he said. "A track-layer. Before I became president of the Valley Spur line, I was a construction foreman."

Nora looked up in surprise. "You? You're the president of the Valley Spur line?"

"But you are so young. I thought railroad presidents were all old, and fat, and wore a monocle and a goatee."

"Well now, my girl, you have just described the presidents of *successful* lines."

"But even so, to be the president of a railroad. My, that's very impressive. Of course, it would be even more impressive if it were a line that had regular train service. I would love to see the trains running in Jordan Valley again."

"Perhaps they will," Pat said.

"You mean there's a chance train service will start

again?"

"Yes. I'm going to Boise now to meet with the board of directors of the Great Western Bank. If I am successful, you'll have your train service."

"Do you have a plan?" Nora asked. "I read in one of my business courses that banks don't like to lend money, unless there is a plan with a chance of success."

"I'll verify that your book is correct on that point," Pat said, "but the truth is, I do have a plan. The problem is that the bank thinks much as you were thinking a moment ago. They aren't certain that someone my age and with my lack of experience can run a railroad. I have to convince them that I can do it."

"How did you become the president of the railroad?" Nora asked.

"I elected myself," Pat replied, smiling broadly.

"You elected yourself?"

"Sure. I am the major stockholder, so I called a stockholders' meeting of one and nominated myself. Then I elected myself president."

"How did you go from being a construction engineer to becoming the major stockholder in the Valley Spur line?" Nora asked.

"I found little glory in the army," Pat said. "So, when my enlistment was up, I left. Lucky for me, too, as you know what happened to Custer at the Little Big Horn. After that, I served on a ship for a while, carrying tea from China. Then I drove a stagecoach some, punched a few cows, followed my father's line of work and served as a lawman. I even did some gold mining."

"Oh, did you find any gold?"

Pat pulled out a rawhide cord that hung around his neck under his shirt. A nugget was suspended from the cord.

"This is all the gold I found," he said. "I call it my lucky nugget because I swore to stick with mining until I found gold. It wasn't much, but it satisfied my vow and let me get out of there."

"Then you went into the railroad business?"

"Yes, I took a job as construction engineer for the Valley Spur line, taking much of my pay in stock. By the time the railroad went broke, I held three-hundred fifty-one shares, which made me the second majority stockholder. Rather than see the railroad go under, I bought six-hundred-fifty shares from the other members of the board of directors, and that gave me a thousand and one shares, making me the majority shareholder for the entire company."

"Given all that you have told me, do you think it was wise of you to buy all those shares? It must have been very expensive."

"It was six-hundred-fifty dollars, which in the scope of things wasn't all that expensive, but as to whether it was the wise thing to do, that we shall soon find out," Pat said. "If I can convince the bank to go with me, it was wise of me to buy the shares. If I can't, it was most unwise, for I'll wind up with nothing." They returned to the engine and Pat climbed aboard, then helped Nora up. She took the basket from him and put it back in the chest, while he threw several chunks of wood into the firebox.

Nora watched him, enjoying the easy grace of his motion and the restrained strength of his arms and shoulders.

"Mr. Flannigan?"

"Yes?" Pat said, looking over toward her as he poked at the roaring fire.

"You'll make it," Nora said. "I know you will."

"Well, I thank you for your vote of confidence," Pat said. He opened the throttle, and the train started forward again.

Nora leaned back on her seat and watched the rails rush toward them. She listened to the clack of the rail joints and the powerful throb of the engine, and before she knew it, she was asleep.

"We're here," Pat said.

Nora had been sleeping, and she was startled by Pat's hand on her shoulder.

"What is it?" Nora asked. "What's wrong?"

"Nothing's wrong," Pat replied. "I just thought you might want to know that we are here."

Nora rubbed her eyes and looked out the window. She saw a depot building, a platform, and a freight warehouse, and knew she was at a rail yard, though the train was not where it would normally be when one arrived at a station.

"I'm not a scheduled operation," Pat explained, seeing the look of confusion on Nora's face. "I had to come through the switches to the most out-of-the-way track. The depot is over there." He pointed.

Nora stood up and stretched. "Can't we go on to Jordan Valley? I know we have track there."

"It's going to take a bit of finagling before I can actually start service, but I expect to be able to do so within another couple of weeks."

"Another couple of weeks," Nora repeated.

"I'm afraid so."

Nora chuckled. "Well, I have no intention of remaining here for two weeks to be able to catch the next train, so I'll take your leave now, and finish my trip by stagecoach. I do, however appreciate the ride more than I can say," Nora said.

"And I appreciated the company," Pat replied. "Here's

an idea. How about you allowing me to buy you dinner in Jordan Valley two weeks from now?"

"Mr. Flannigan..."

"Pat."

"Pat, if you can actually get service established to Jordan Valley two weeks from now, I'll accept your invitation."

CHAPTER THREE

Nora was ready to board the stagecoach by six o'clock the next morning.

"Looks like you're goin' to be the only passenger this mornin', Miss," he looked at the ticket, "Cassidy."

"What time will we get there, Mister..."

"Sam, just call me Sam. We'll be there by four o'clock, this afternoon. We'll be changin' teams at nine, and we'll stop for lunch around one and change teams again, and then if all goes well, we should be pullin' into the valley by four o'clock. But seein' as you're the only passenger, if you need to stop for any...uh...reason, just give me a shout and I'll be happy to stop for you."

Nora grinned. "Thank you, Sam, I'm sure I'll be just fine."

Sam loaded Nora's baggage into the boot, then helped her into the coach. A moment later she heard a loud pop, almost as loud as a gunshot.

"Heah!" Sam shouted, and, with a little jerk, the coach got underway.

The stagecoach was much slower, and quieter than the

train ride had been, especially the part of her train ride that had included time in the engine.

She thought about Pat Flannigan. One-time soldier, sailor, stagecoach driver, cowboy, prospector, construction engineer on the railroad, and now majority shareholder and president of that railroad. She had to admit, that he had to be one of the most interesting men she had ever met.

She was enjoying the pace of the stagecoach ride because it gave her time for a leisurely enjoyment of the countryside. And, because she was the only passenger, she was able to slide from side to side to enjoy whichever view most appealed to her.

For a while, the stagecoach road was running parallel to the railroad tracks. Valley Spur tracks. She found herself sincerely hoping that Pat Flannigan would make a success of the railroad, and not just for him, but also because of the benefit returning rail service to the county.

When the coach stopped in front of the Jordan Valley stage depot, the following cloud of dust roiled past the windows.

"Here we are, Miss Cassidy, all safe and sound," the driver called down.

"Thanks, Sam," Nora called back.

The newspaper office was a block away from the stage depot, and when she stepped inside, she saw her father wiping down the platen of the Washington Hand Press he used to publish the *Jordan Valley Monitor.*

"Nora!" he called happily, looking up as she stepped through the front door.

"Papa!"

Nora started toward her father, with her arms spread wide.

Sterling held his hands up, palm out to stop her. "No,

honey, I've got printer's ink on my apron."

"I love printer's ink," Nora replied with a little laugh, giving him a hug, anyway.

They took their supper that evening in the dining room of the Morning Star Hotel. Several citizens of the town stopped by to welcome Nora home, and it was well into their meal before Nora was able to tell her father what she had been waiting to say.

"Papa, we're getting rail service back," she said, enthusiastically.

"I'm afraid not, darlin'," Sterling replied. "The railroad wasn't able to make it profitable, so they went out of business."

"No, Patrick Flannigan bought the other major stockholders out, and now he's the majority shareholder. He's going to reopen the railroad."

"Who is this Patrick Flannigan person?"

Nora told her father how he had enough shares of stock, to be able to take control of the railroad.

"He's going to start service to Jordan Valley again," she said excitedly.

"Nora, girl, you have just given me the next article for the *Monitor*."

From the Jordan Valley Monitor
Rail Service to Return to Jordan Valley

> *Word has reached this newspaper that a resourceful young man by the name of Patrick Flannigan has secured controlling interest in the Valley Spur Railroad. It is his intention to renew service*

to our city and county.

If Mr. Flannigan is successful, in his enterprise, it can't but be to the advantage of every man, woman, and child in the county. To our ranchers, it will be a source of getting their cattle to market. To our businessmen, it will be a source of re-supply. And to everyone else it will be an open door to the rest of our nation. Newspapers from New York will reach us in a timely manner. To the adventuresome traveler who would wish to go to Chicago, St. Louis, New York, Boston, or our nation's capital, the trip can be made in a matter of days, rather than weeks.

The late afternoon sun speared through the window, illuminating millions of dust motes, and splashing pools of light on the highly polished conference table. Four men sat on one side of the table, and Pat Flannigan sat on the other side. He fingered his gold nugget as he studied the board members. Each of the four men had a folder of papers, and they shuffled through them importantly. One, a large man with heavy white muttonchop whiskers, polished his glasses, then put them on and stared across the table at Pat. His name was Emmett Noland, and he was the chairman of the board.

"Mr. Flannigan, our final figures have been compiled," he said. He cleared his throat. "The cash we received from the sale of all moveable stock, plus the sale of the office buildings here in Boise, and the sale of the buildings and furnishings in Portland, came to a grand total of $458,384.17. We have applied that to the debt the Valley Spur line owes this bank, leaving a balance due of $41,615.83. The current value of your holdings, to include all fixed assets such as track, bridges, grading, etcetera, and the single engine and ten passenger cars, five freight cars and twenty-five cattle cars you have insisted upon retaining, comes to a little over $100,000. Technically, Mr. Flannigan, your assets are now greater than your liabilities."

Pat grinned broadly. "Then I'm in business?"

"Not exactly," Noland said. "We have looked over your plan of operation, and we find one rather substantial flaw."

"What flaw have you found?" Pat asked.

"It's the land grant property, Mr. Flannigan. You are planning to use it to improve the position of the railroad, but the land has not officially been transferred into your hands."

"It will be on June 30th," Pat said.

"Only if railroad service is reestablished by that time," Noland said. "If you don't have regular service on a scheduled basis by June 30th, the land reverts to the United States government."

"I'm aware of that," Pat said. "Service will be reestablished by June 30th."

"Mr. Flannigan," Noland said. He rubbed his hand through his hair and looked at Pat, as if forced to explain something to a child. "This is June 22nd. What makes you think you can have scheduled service established by the 30th?"

"I will do it," Pat said simply. "Provided I get the support I need from you gentlemen."

Noland cleared his throat. "You have asked for one hundred thousand dollars."

"Yes," Pat said.

"That's quite impossible. The government grant land

cannot be used as collateral, and you don't have $100,000 worth of property."

"I don't understand," Pat said. "You just said my total worth was $100,000."

"From that, you must subtract the nearly $42,000 you owe. And you must also consider that much of that is non-recoverable. The only thing that can be converted to cash is the..." Noland looked at the folder in front of him. "The Nora Cassidy Special."

"No," Pat said. "That is the only locomotive I have. Without it, I have no business at all."

"We realize that," Noland said, "so we are willing to make this proposition to you. We will accept the Nora Cassidy Special as collateral for a loan of $10,000."

"Ten thousand dollars?" Pat said. He sighed. "That's not much money, is it?"

"It depends on how you look at it," Noland said. "If you have to raise it, it's a great deal of money. If you are going to try to operate a railroad on it, it's very little."

"Ten thousand dollars," Pat said again. He sighed and fingered his gold nugget for a moment. "All right, I'll do it. When you get right down to it, I really don't have any choice."

"Mr. Flannigan, I do hope you fully understand the provisions of this loan," Noland said. "You must repay one-fourth of the loan within three months from the time you accept it, and the next installment is due three months later. If you miss one payment, the Nora Cassidy Special can be taken away from you."

"Yes," Pat said. "I understand. Where do I sign?"

Noland slid a paper across the table and showed Pat where to sign. Attached to the paper was a bank draft for ten thousand dollars, made out to Patrick Flannigan, president of the Valley Spur Railroad line.

Pat signed the paper, then took the draft. He put the draft in his pocket and stood up, then shook the hand of each of the board members.

"Gentlemen, it has been a pleasure doing business with you," he said.

"I hope our next meeting is just as pleasant," Noland replied.

James Wilson sat on a fallen tree trunk, eating beans and bacon from his mess skillet. There were half a dozen other men sitting around, enjoying the same fare. In the middle of the group a campfire blazed, pushing back the night. Out in the darkness a frightened calf bawled for its mother and was answered with a reassuring call. The same fire that had cooked the beans and bacon now warmed a pot of coffee, suspended from a rod which was strung out over the fire.

"Tell me, boss," Leo Collins said, wiping up the last of the bean juice with his fingers and a small piece of bread. "When you was a 'dandyin' around in San Francisco 'n all over the place, did you ever eat this well?"

The others laughed at Collins, and James laughed with them as he picked up some sand to clean his plate.

"I never did, Collins," he replied. "I tried to get some beans and bacon at the Mark Hopkins Hotel, but they only wanted to serve pheasant under glass."

"Don't that glass get in your teeth?" Collins asked seriously.

The others laughed at Collins, then one of them asked, "Is they lots of pretty girls in them fancy hotels?"

"If they was, it's my guess the boss had his share," Collins said.

James walked over to slide his mess skillet in his saddlebag. He was twenty-eight, dark and handsome, in a fine-featured way. Until a year ago, he had been a wealthy playboy, spending the generous allowance his father provided for him, in the gaming halls and pleasure palaces of San Francisco and Seattle. It was to this life that the cowboys had been referring.

That was all behind James now. His father had died during the winter, and James had inherited Buckthorn Ranch, the largest and most productive ranch in the entire county. The energy James had once invested in having a good time was now invested in running his ranch. His father had correctly guessed that letting James "sow a few wild oats in his youth" would settle him for the serious days ahead.

"I bet none of them city gals is as pretty as our Mattie Andrews."

"I can't say as I have noticed," James answered. "Mattie is a very pretty girl, but she's running her father's ranch, and she's been all business every time I've been around her."

"You're blind, then, boss."

"You're all blind iffin you haven't taken no notice of Professor Cassidy's daughter. You know the one I'm a'talkin' about? She's just come back from the east. I think she was goin' to school out there or somethin'. That's about the prettiest girl I ever seen anywhere."

There was the sound of an approaching horse, and the men looked up to see a rider coming into the golden bubble of light cast by the campfire.

"Hello, Sweeney," James said. "There are some beans and bacon left."

Sweeney pulled the saddle off his horse, then took out

his mess skillet. He carried it over to ladle some beans up from the pot. He tore off a piece of bread, then walked over and sat down to eat before he said a word. He had been riding nighthawk, a title given the riders who watched over the herd at night.

"It's a fine thing, us sittin' here eatin' beans," Sweeney finally said, "when there's a squatter somewhere who's eatin' Buckthorn beef."

"Eating Buckthorn beef? What do you mean?" James asked.

"I found one of our steers," Sweeney said. Sweeney, like all the cowboys, took a proprietary point of view about everything belonging to the Buckthorn Ranch, so saying "our steer" came easily for him.

"You found one of our steers on squatter land?" Ladner asked. "Did you bring him back?"

"Weren't nothin' to bring back," Sweeney said. "He'd been slaughtered, 'n' there wasn't nothin' left but head and hide. The meat was all took."

"Damn it," James said, striking his hand with his fist.

"I tracked whoever done it," Sweeney went on. "The tracks led across Bender Creek, 'n' onto the railroad grant land. You know what that means."

"Boss, they ain't nobody but squatters livin' on the railroad grant land," Ladner said.

"If you ask me, we need to pay them folks a little visit," Collins said.

"Yeah," Ladner added. "And we can take a couple of torches along too. You know, as sort of a callin' card?"

"No," James said. "We aren't going to do anything like that."

"But, boss, we can't let them get away with butcherin' our beef," Ladner insisted. "If they tell other squatters they butchered one of our beeves 'n' got away with it, the first thing you know we'll be feedin' all the sodbusters in the whole valley."

"They aren't going to get away with it," James said. "I'll go see the Sheriff Ferrell tomorrow. Butchering someone else's steer is grand larceny."

"Grand larceny, yeah," Collins said. "Maybe the law will hang the son-of-a-bitch. It's been a long time since I was to a public hangin'. They're more fun than a county fair."

"You ain't gonna see no hangin'," Ladner said.

"They's fences too," Sweeney said.

"Fences? What do you mean?" James asked.

"Them sodbusters have put up fences, all along this side of the creek. Our cows can't even get to the water."

"Damn it!" James said. "That's railroad grant land. It's still in dispute because there isn't even a railroad running here anymore. The squatters have no right to fence it off."

"That's what I was thinkin'," Sweeney said. "But they claim our cattle get into their fields and destroy their crops. Leastwise, that's what the fella said who was standin' guard by the fence."

"You mean there was someone standing guard?" James asked.

"Yep. He seen me drop a rope over one of the poles, commencin' to jerk the fence out, 'n' he come out there with a scattergun 'n' ask me to leave."

"What'd you do?" Ladner asked.

"I left," Sweeney said easily. "Any more coffee?"

Collins nodded and Sweeney got up and poured a cup of the steaming black liquid into his cup. He sucked it through extended lips and looked at the others. "What would you have done?" Sweeney asked.

"Iffen a fella come up to me with a scattergun 'n'

asked me to leave, why, I reckon I'd leave," Collins said in a voice which let it be known that no one blamed Sweeney. "But that still don't give that squatter the right to be there in the first place. Boss, we ain't gonna let 'em get away with this, are we?"

"The wheat field, down by the breaks," James said, "it isn't fenced, is it?"

"No," Sweeney said. "Our cows don't generally wander down there. I guess the sodbusters figured there was no need for it."

"They figured wrong," James said. "Saddle up, men. We're going to move our herd."

"Now you're a'talkin', boss," Ladner said.

"You'd think they'd learn, wouldn't you?" Collins asked.

CHAPTER FOUR

Nora had been home for a week and was fully into her work on the newspaper. She stepped back and looked at the page plate which had occupied her morning, but now the type was set, and needed only to be put on the press to print the paper. The type was set backwards, but Nora's eye was so practiced that she could read it easily, and she proofed the dateline: June 27, 1881, Jordan Valley, Oregon.

Behind Nora her father worked on the press, making adjustments here, wiping it with a cleaning rag there. He pampered it and treated it almost as if it were a living thing. Though the big city dailies had steam operated presses which could turn out thousands of copies an hour, the *Valley Monitor* still depended upon a hand operated, flat plate printing press. It was adequate for their needs.

"Ra, did you read the Polecat column?" Sterling asked his daughter.

"I read it as I was setting the copy," Nora replied.

"That's no way to read an editorial," Sterling chided. "It should be read slowly, so that every word has meaning."

Nora laughed. "Papa, you act as if the Polecat column is a work of art."

"It is, Ra," Sterling replied seriously. "On, not the writing itself, mind you. I make no bones about my writing ability. I'm just a simple country newspaper man. But the *art*, Ra, is in the fact that it exists at all. I've attacked the United States government for not being more decisive with the railroad grant lands. I feel they should either turn title over to the railroad, so the railroad could sell the land to raise much needed revenue, or they should take the lands back so the cattlemen could buy it. They definitely should *not* leave the lands in limbo, so the squatters can move in."

"Do you think the government will listen?" Nora asked.

"I don't know," Sterling admitted. "But it's a wonderful country, where a citizen can attack his own government in print, and not fear reprisals."

"Who are the squatters, Papa?" Nora asked. "How did they get out here on the railroad land?"

"They came by wagon train," Sterling said. "Two years ago, a wagon train bound for Portland was snowed in here, and they had to spend the winter. The folks hereabout took pity on them. They supplied them with food, shared their water, even sponsored a dance to raise money for them. But when the snows cleared, the wagon train didn't move on. The squatters learned that the land they were on was in dispute, and they figured they had the right to stay as long as they wanted."

"What's wrong with that?" Nora asked.

"Well, to begin with, it's not legal," Sterling said. "No one can settle there until after the 30th of this month, when the railroad loses title."

Nora thought of Pat Flannigan and his plans to save the railroad.

"Do you think the railroad will lose the land?" she asked.

"If your friend, Patrick, isn't able to re-establish service before then, then, yes, the railroad will lose the land grants," Sterling said.

"But you wrote an article about him reopening the railroad."

"Yes, and I had hopes that he would, but," he sighed, then went to his desk and held up a telegram, "I got this telegram yesterday, and I didn't want to upset you with the news. But I have since learned that Flannigan didn't get as much money from the bank as he had hoped."

"Oh," Nora said sadly. "So you think he won't be able to reopen the railroad?"

"I fear not."

"That's too bad because he was such a nice man," Nora said. "I feel sorry for him, and for the citizens of the valley. I was just thinking of how nice it would be to have rail service again."

"Oh, I've no doubt but that eventually, it will come," Sterling assured her. "No one is going to dig up the tracks, and as long as they are here, someone will come along and use them. Perhaps another, more established railroad, which can afford to absorb the loss of revenue until it becomes a paying operation."

"Papa, what will happen to the land if the railroad loses it?"

"The cattlemen have first claim," Sterling said. "You see, every one of the ranchers is now running more cattle than they can actually support with the grass and water that they currently own. So, they've had to resort to using the railroad grant lands. Now that's worked out just fine, because there's been enough to go around. But the squatters have moved in, and with their fences, they've cut off the water and the grass. This is ranching country and anything that hurts the ranchers, hurts the economy of all of us. That's why I think the government should run the squatters off."

"Where would they go?" Nora asked.

"Well, they could go to wherever they were headed in the first place," another voice said, and startled, Nora and Sterling looked around to see a man standing just on the other side of the counter.

"James," Sterling said. "I didn't hear you come in."

"Hello, Professor," James Wilson said. He took off his hat and smiled engagingly at Nora. "Hello, Nora, welcome home."

"Hello, James," Nora replied.

"What can I do for you?" Sterling asked.

"I want some posters printed. You know the kind, like the wanted posters the law puts out when they offer a reward for someone."

"Wanted posters? Are you putting out a reward on someone?"

"No," James said, "I just want that kind of a poster. I want it to say: 'Warning. This is cattle range land. Fences or any other obstruction to water and grass will be removed by force.' I want it big enough so that a fellow can read it from quite a distance."

"Do you think that will have any effect on the squatters?" Sterling asked.

"I really don't know," James said, "but I've got to give it a try."

"Are they giving you any more trouble?"

"They butchered one of my beeves last night. I was going to report it to the sheriff, but I decided to let it go this time. I really don't know who took it. Besides, they only took one, and they didn't take it to sell, because they took the meat. I guess they were hungry."

"If you ask me, James, you are just too good to them. They have no business out there in the first place," Sterling said.

"I'm hoping these posters will do the trick," James said. "I'm going to post them everywhere; then I'm going to tear down every fence, gate, water flume, and grain storage building I see."

"I'll have them ready by tomorrow morning," Sterling promised. "Is that soon enough?"

"Yes," James said. "I can have them all posted by tomorrow afternoon, and still have time for the Cowboys' Dance tomorrow night. You remember the cowboy dances, don't you, Nora?"

"How could I forget the dances at the Morning Star Hotel?" Nora replied. "Papa used to let me go, but he wouldn't let me dance because he said I was too young."

"You aren't too young now," James said, "and I would be awfully pleased if you'd let me escort you tomorrow night."

"Ra would be happy to go with you, James. What time will you call for her?" Sterling asked.

"I'll be here at seven," James said. He put his hat back on, smiled, then left.

Nora waited until he was gone before she spoke.

"Why didn't you let me speak for myself?" Nora asked.

"I didn't know what you would say," Sterling admitted. "I wanted you to say yes, so I just said it for you."

"Oh? Just try and keep me away," Nora teased. "Those summer dances are about the closest thing to a social life we have in Jordan Valley. I'm going, all right. It's just that in the future, Papa, let me arrange my own dates, all right?"

"I'll try to remember that," Sterling promised.

Mattie Andrews rose up from the smell of burnt hair and flesh and looked down at the calf she had just branded. She rubbed her soft brown hair away from her forehead and glanced toward the holding pen with flashing blue eyes. She was a very pretty, young woman, though she insisted on wearing the same jeans and shirt outfits that the cowboys on her ranch wore.

Mattie Andrews was twenty-three, and it was legend among not only her ranch hands, but the ranch hands of the entire valley, that she could rope and brand as well as any man, and ride better than anyone. For the last six years, Mattie had won the Independence Day horse race, and the odds were strongly in favor of her winning again this year.

"Miss Mattie, there's only about three more of the little critters that need a mark," Willie, her foreman, said. "If you want to take a break, I can finish up for you."

"No, thank you, Willie," Mattie said. "I'll finish." Mattie put the branding iron back in the fire. Then she saw a rider approaching. She shielded her eyes from the sun and stared for a moment, then she smiled broadly. "On second thought, if you don't mind, I will let you finish."

Willie looked up, surprised at Mattie's sudden change of mind. Then he saw the rider too, and he understood. James Wilson was dropping by for a visit.

James Wilson's father and Mattie's father had settled the rangeland years before. James's father had died a few years earlier, and Mattie's father had been injured in an accident, though he was still alive and as active as he could be, although he had to use a cane.

Buck Andrews had also seen James approaching, and by the time Mattie was out of the cattle pen, Buck had hobbled down from the house, and father and daughter met their visitor by the outside well.

James swung down from his horse, greeted both of them, and took a drink of water before he spoke.

"Well, James, what brings you over here?" Buck asked.

"I've come to ask you if you'll throw your weight behind a campaign I'm starting," James said, flinging the last few drops of water from the dipper, then replacing the dipper on the hook.

"What kind of campaign?"

"I was just into the newspaper office, and I'm having some posters printed," James said. "They're going to be a warning to all squatters that the railroad grant land is cattle range land. The posters are going to say how we're going to tear down all fences and the like which would interfere with cattle getting to water or grass."

"By damn, it's about time somebody did somethin' about these squatters," Buck said. "You're mighty right. I'll back you."

"Good," James said. "That's good, Mr. Andrews. When the others hear you're behind it, too, we'll have a hundred percent cooperation in the valley."

"Are you going into town on the Fourth of July?" Mattie asked James.

"On the Fourth? I don't know, why?" James asked.

"Oh, no reason," Mattie said, her face reflected a little disappointment.

James smiled. "Oh, you must mean for your race," he said. "I guess I might as well. After all, I've bet a hundred dollars on you to win."

"Really?" Mattie said, smiling brightly. Then she frowned. "Oh, James, I hope I don't let you down."

"You won't let me down. Oh, by the way, guess who I'm taking to the dance tomorrow night?"

"Who?" Mattie asked, brushing the hair from her forehead with a nervous gesture.

"An old friend of yours," James said.

"An old friend of mine?"

"Yes," James said. "You remember Nora Cassidy, don't you? It seems to me that I remember the two of you being very close."

"Oh, yes," Mattie said easily. "We were very good friends, and I feel just terrible for not getting in town to see her before now. I've been so busy with the ranch..."

"Mattie is practically running it for me now," Buck put in. "I've been worthless as a plug mule ever since I smashed up my leg."

"Nonsense," Mattie said. "I'm helping you, but I'm certainly not running the ranch."

James smiled. "That's not what I hear," he said. "I hear you're about the best rancher in the valley."

"That's the truth," Buck said. "That's the absolute truth."

"Well, if you haven't seen Nora since she returned, maybe you'll get a chance to see her tomorrow night," James suggested.

"Tomorrow night?"

"At the dance."

"Oh, well, I probably won't be going to the dance," Mattie said. "I've got so much to do here, and I really don't care much for those silly things. You know how it is."

"Why, Mattie Andrews, I've heard you say two or three times this week how you were looking forward to going," Buck said.

"Well, not really the dance part," Mattie said. "I was just looking forward to getting into town."

"If you get into town, try and make it to the dance,"

James said.

"I'll try," Mattie promised.

James swung back onto his horse. "And, Mr. Andrews, it's good to hear that you'll support my poster campaign." He touched the brim of his hat. "See you."

Buck and Mattie watched him ride off, then Buck spoke.

"You know, when Louis was alive, he and I use to think that maybe..." he let his voice trail off.

"Maybe what, Papa?"

"That you and James would someday..." he scoffed and made a waving motion with his hand. "Ah, it was just two old men talking, is all."

CHAPTER FIVE

The Morning Star Hotel was the biggest hotel in Jordan Valley. In fact, if one didn't count the Widow Murphy's house, which she converted into a small hotel after her husband died, the Morning Star was the only hotel in Jordan Valley. It was three stories high, with nine rooms on each of the top two floors, and a restaurant and ballroom on the ground floor.

Every Saturday night during the summer, the ballroom was taken over by the Valley Cattlemen's Association for the Cowboys' Dance. The dance was free to all comers, and it was, as Nora had told her father, the biggest social event in Jordan Valley.

Excitement would begin to build Saturday morning, when the stagecoach would arrive with the band. The children of the town would start gathering around the stage depot about half an hour before the stage was due, laughing, pulling each other's hair, sometimes breaking into a dance of their own. They pretended to be the band, strumming imaginary guitars, and playing phantom fiddles and accordions.

A few of the cowboys would drift by casually, as if they

had other business to attend to and just happened to be in the area. The young women would drop into the general store, just next door to the depot, where they would buy brightly colored ribbons or notions, pretending an innocence of the fact that the band was at that very moment unloading their instruments. On many such mornings last-minute adjustments to dance cards were arranged by the "chance" meetings.

The arrival of the stage would first be announced by the driver's trumpet. He would sound it as soon as the stage crossed the bridge, far down in the valley, and its clear, brassy tone would carry into town, alerting everyone, so that by the time the coach and six rolled down Main Street, nearly half the town had turned out.

Nora stood in the window of the newspaper office, watching as the stage stopped, and the four men of the band climbed out, then began taking their instruments down. They realized they were the center of much attention, and they moved importantly, engrossed in the work of unloading, seemingly taking no notice of the excitement their arrival had caused.

"How do they look?" Sterling called from the press. He was preparing the plates for the printing of the posters James had ordered.

"Who?" Nora asked.

Sterling laughed. "The band, of course. Do you think I don't know why you're looking out the window?"

Nora smiled and came away from the window. She picked up the poster stock and put it in place for the printing. "The band looks fine," she said. "It'll be a fine dance."

"Good, good," Sterling said. "Your first dance after returning home should be a nice dance. If I thought the prettiest girl in the valley would save at least one dance for

---

her father, I might even be persuaded to go."

"Oh, I'm terribly sorry, Father, but my dance card is filled with big fish," Nora teased. Sterling laughed, then twisted the handle of the press, and the first poster was done.

The wagon drew to a stop by the edge of the wheat field. There were two men in the wagon, one very large man with a full beard, and the other, a younger version of the large man. The men were Johan Forsberg, and his seventeen-year-old son, Lars.

"Jumping jeehosifat, Pop, what happened to our wheat?" Lars asked.

The field before them was mashed flat, with the just-budding heads trampled in the ground. Johan had seen fields like this before, after a hail, storm, and once, back east, during the Civil War, when an army moved through.

"I don't know, boy," he said.

Johan got down from the wagon and walked over to the edge of the field. He bent to one knee and picked up a handful of dirt and straw. Ten acres of wheat totally destroyed! It was a mystery, until he saw the cow droppings and hoof marks.

Johan stood up and stuck his hands deep into his bib overall pockets and looked out across the valley. Far in the distance, he could see the herds staying near the grass and water. The question was, what brought them up here to the wheat field? There was no water for them. They wouldn't have come unless... suddenly Johan realized what had happened, and he spit angrily upon the ground.

"They were driven," he said resolutely.

"What'd you say, Pop?" Lars asked.

"Those cows were driven into our wheat fields," Johan

said. "Now what'd they wanna go 'n' do that for? This part of the valley over here isn't in dispute."

"I don't know, Pop, the cattlemen do some things just for pure meanness," Lars said.

Johan started back toward the wagon when he noticed something he hadn't seen before. A white poster was attached to a nearby tree. He walked over and pulled it down, then read it.

"They got no right," he said angrily.

"What is that, Pop?"

Johan held the poster up for his son to see.

WARNING
To all Squatters
Any fence-line or other
Construction that limits
Cattle access to grass or water
Will be destroyed

"The cattlemen say they are goin' to tear down all our construction in the grant lands. They got no right to do that."

"They don't need right on their side," Lars said. "This is cow country 'n' everybody seems to be on the cowman's side."

Johan folded up the poster and put it in his pocket.

"I know what we could do," Lars said. "We could butcher a cow every time they tear down one of our fences."

"No," Johan said emphatically. "That'd put the law on their side for sure. Butcherin' a steer is a jailin' offense. Tearin' down a fence is just like spittin' on the street. 'Bout the most can happen is a fine, 'n then the fine goes to the gov'ment, 'n' not the fella who got his fence torn down. If they caught us butcherin' a steer, they could shoot us dead, and no one would blame 'em. It's too dangerous."

"It's not dangerous at all," Lars said. "I killed one yesterday morning, and never heard a word about it."

"What?" Johan asked, looking at his son in shock. "Did you just say you killed a steer yesterday?"

"Killed it, skinned it, and took the meat," Lars said proudly.

"I'm goin' into town tonight," Johan said. "And I'm gonna pay for the steer you butchered. It'll take every thing we have left."

"Pop, what are you gonna do that for?" Lars asked. "We *deserve* that meat, after all they've put us through."

"Boy, I guess I just been flappin' my gums around you twenty years for nothing," Johan said as he urged the team on. "You haven't learned anything, have you?"

By dusk, the excitement which had been growing for the entire day in Jordan Valley was full blown. The sound of the practicing musicians could be heard all up and down Main Street. Children gathered around the glowing, yellow windows, and peered inside. The dance floor was cleared of all tables and chairs, and the musicians had been installed on the platform at the front of the room.

The band started two or three numbers, *Buffalo Gals, The Gandy Dancers' Ball,* and *Little Joe the Wrangler,* being the most popular. Horses and buckboards began arriving and soon every hitching rail on Main Street was full. Men and women streamed along the boardwalks toward the hotel, the women in colorful ginghams, the men in clean, blue denims and brightly decorated vests.

James arrived promptly at seven at the Cassidy house, which was located at the opposite end of Main Street from the newspaper office. He was wearing a tan suit and highly polished boots, with a dark silk vest covering a white frilled shirt.

"James, you do know how to turn out," Sterling said, as James stepped into the house.

"I try," James said as Nora came into the room. "Are you ready to go? The dance has already started."

"I've been waiting all day," Nora said, "but I must warn you some of my dances are promised."

"Oh?" James replied. The expression on his face showed that he didn't care for that idea.

"To my father," Nora added with a small laugh.

James smiled broadly. "Oh, your *father.* Well, as long as your father is the *only* other person on your dance card."

Nora walked between James and her father, as they went to the hotel. Even before they arrived, they were able to feel some of the excitement, for the hotel was aglow with light, and bubbling over with conversation and laughter.

The high skirling of the fiddle could be heard, even from a block away.

Once inside, the excitement was all it promised to be. Young women in butterfly bright dresses and men in denim and leather laughed and talked. To one side of the dance floor there was a large punchbowl on a table. Nora watched one of the cowboys walk over to the punchbowl and, unobtrusively, he poured whiskey into the punch from a bottle he had concealed beneath his vest. A moment later another cowboy did the same thing, and Nora smiled as she thought of the potency of the punch.

The music was playing, but as yet, no one was dancing. Then the music stopped, and one of the players lifted a megaphone.

"Choose up your squares!" the caller shouted. The cowboys started toward the young women, who, giggling and turning their faces away shyly, accepted their invitations. In a moment there were three squares formed and waiting. Nora and James were in the square nearest the band, and as she looked across the square, she saw Mattie Andrews.

"Mattie!" Nora squealed, and the two women rushed together and embraced quickly.

"I was wondering, when you were going to see me," Mattie said. "I saw you the moment you walked in. Of course, everyone saw you. You look simply wonderful."

"Oh, don't be silly," Nora said. "Mattie, you must come to see me."

"I will," Mattie promised, and as the caller raised his megaphone, Mattie and Nora moved back to their positions in the square.

The music began, with the fiddles loud and clear, the guitars carrying the rhythm, the accordion providing the counterpoint, and the dobro singing over everything. The caller began to shout, and he clapped his hands and stomped his feet and danced around on the platform in compliance with his own calls, bowing and whirling as if he had a girl and was in one of the squares himself. The dancers moved and swirled to the caller's commands.

Around the dance floor sat those who were without partners, looking on wistfully; those who were too old, holding back those who were too young.

When Nora danced with her father, she noticed that James was dancing with Mattie. If Nora had a best friend in the valley, it would be Mattie, for the two girls, both single children, had grown nearly as close as sisters over the years.

The dance went on into the night, and though a couple of the cowboys who had drunk too much punch got into an argument over the favors of one of the young women, the ruckus was quickly and quietly settled so that nothing disturbed the dancers.

But that peace was disturbed around 10:30, when a large, bearded man, carrying a pitchfork, walked into the ballroom.

"You can't come in here, sodbuster," one of the cowboys called, and started toward him, bent on throwing him out.

The big man shoved the cowboy back with such amazing strength that the cowboy hit the punchbowl table and knocked the bowl onto the floor. It broke with a crashing tinkle of glass, and some of the women let out small shouts of fear and surprise.

"What do you want?" Sterling asked the man. "Why have you come in here to disturb decent folks?"

"I want to see James Wilson," the man said calmly. He spoke in a quiet voice, but it was a deep and rumbling voice which sounded loud in the sudden quiet of the room.

The man was in his mid-to-late forties. He was wearing bibbed overalls and a red shirt. His hat, unlike the stylish, blocked hats of the cowboys, was misshapen and tattered, sweat stained and dirty. He had a full gray beard, and his eyes reflected the light of dozens of lanterns and candles, giving them a demonic glow. His forearms, exposed by the rolled back shirt, bulged with muscle.

James was standing right beside Nora when the man spoke his name. Nora felt James tense, then start toward the middle of the dance floor to confront him.

"Here I am, Mr. Forsberg," James said calmly. "What do you want?"

"Justice," Forsberg said.

"Justice?"

Forsberg pulled a dirty wad of bills from his bib pocket.

"Here is twenty dollars," he said. "They tell me that's what one head will bring in Portland. I'm payin' for the steer my boy Lars killed yesterday mornin'."

There was a buzz of excitement through the room, but then it stopped, as James made no effort to retrieve the money.

"What's the matter?" Forsberg asked. "Isn't squatter money good enough for you?"

"Where'd you steal that money, Forsberg?" one of the cowboys jeered, and the others laughed and made catcalls.

"Well, now, Mr. Forsberg," James said. "It's one thing for you to come up and ask me if you could buy one of my beeves, but it's quite another for you to take it first and pay afterward."

"Yeah," one of the other cowboys called, "that's called rustlin' in this territory."

"I think we oughtta string 'im up!" another shouted, and Forsberg looked around nervously, but he didn't make any effort to leave.

"There's another matter I'd like to discuss with you," Forsberg said. "You ran your cows over my wheat."

"Yes, sir," James said, "I'll confess to doing that."

"I figure I would have made about thirty bushels an acre on that ten acres," Forsberg said. "At thirty cents a bushel, that comes to ninety dollars. I'll deduct this twenty-dollars and you'll owe me seventy."

"Mr. Forsberg, your wheat field was on grazing land," James said.

"My wheat field was on the railroad grant land, Wilson," Forsberg said. "And that means that I have as much right there as you or any of your cows."

"Mr. Forsberg, if you have a few head of cattle, or a few horses you would like to turn out on that land, I don't think anyone in the valley would begrudge you. The cows and horses eat a little grass, drink a little water, then they move on leaving the land and the grass and the water for others. When you plant crops, you fence off the grasslands and the water, and you plough up what you don't fence off. You are taking it all for yourself, and you leave nothing for anyone else."

"I have as much right to that land as anyone, until the government decides what to do with it," Forsberg said. "And not you or anybody else can stop me. And as for these things," Forsberg pulled a crumpled poster from his bib pocket and Nora recognized it as one of the posters she and her father had printed for James. "You know what you can do with these things?" Forsberg shouted angrily.

"I'm glad you noticed them," James said calmly. "Now there will be no question when we start taking down your fences."

"You aren't takin' down any fences of mine, sir!" Forsberg shouted. He lunged at James with the pitchfork.

Nora, frightened that James would be killed, screamed, "James, look out!"

James saw Forsberg lunge toward him, and, at the last second, he managed to lean away just as the tines of the pitchfork slipped by. He grabbed for the handle of the pitchfork, but Forsberg was a powerful bull of a man and he managed to jerk the pitchfork back, pulling it free from James's hands. Forsberg laughed evilly and lunged again, but again James managed to dance lightly to one side.

"Stop them!" Nora called. "Somebody please stop them!" But even as she yelled, she knew that James was on his own, and she bit her lips and hung on the edge of stark terror as she watched the angry giant try to kill the man who had brought her to the dance.

Forsberg had the advantage in strength, but James was more agile, and this time, instead of trying to grab the handle, James hit Forsberg in the face with his fist. He was well set, and he put a lot of power behind his swing. Forsberg, who was concentrating on thrusting the pitchfork, didn't see the blow coming, and James caught him squarely on the nose.

Forsberg let out a bellow of pain, and a small trickle of blood began oozing from his nose. James felt the nose go under his fist, and he knew he had broken it. And yet, amazingly, Forsberg didn't go down. Instead, with a roar which exposed his teeth, now stained red with the blood which ran across his mouth and into his beard, Forsberg made still another lunge.

"Knock him down, James!" one of the cowboys shouted in a lusty cheer, and James, wondering just what it would take to knock him down, caught Forsberg with another solid blow, this time aimed for the Adam's apple. That one did the trick, and Forsberg dropped the pitchfork, then grabbed his neck and fell to his knees, gagging and choking and trying to breathe.

"You've got 'im, Jamey!" someone else shouted. "Now finish him off!"

James stepped up to Forsberg and drew back his fist for one more blow, then he held it for a moment and finally let his arms drop to his side.

"Mr. Fisher?" James called quietly.

"Yes, James?"

"I'm going to write out a draft to Mr. Forsberg for seventy dollars. When he brings it to the bank Monday morning, I would like you to honor it without question."

"Very well, James," the banker said.

"Now, Mr. Forsberg, you have recovered the loss of your wheat, sir. Now, if you would, please leave, as you are disturbing folks who just want to have a good time."

Forsberg stood up, still clutching his neck. He looked at James with a face red from the struggle and his anger. James finished writing out the draft and handed it to the big man. Forsberg took it sullenly and put it in his pocket without saying a word.

"Don't bother to thank me," James said easily. "But be prepared, Mr. Forsberg, because your fences *are* coming down."

Forsberg started to reach for his pitchfork, but James put his foot over the handle. "You can pick it up Monday, when you come to the bank," he said. "Good evening, Mr. Forsberg."

Forsberg scowled at James, then at the others. Finally, he left the room and the men and women in the room cheered for James.

"Music!" James called. "We have more dancing yet."

About half an hour before the dance was over Professor Cassidy said that he was tired, and he left. When the dance finally did end, Nora and James walked home alone. It was a beautiful evening, and the moon was in a quarter phase, so that the stars were even more brilliant.

"I certainly missed our starry evening skies when I was away," Nora said.

"You had the same stars back east," James teased.

"No, I think not," Nora said. "They were but pale imitations of these. See how they glisten? It's almost as if the taller trees are holding them in place, they seem that close."

"I'm glad you like them so," James said. "Perhaps it will keep you here."

"James, that was a nice thing you did back there at the dance," Nora said. "Other, lesser men would have beaten him and thrown him out without a thing. You paid for his crop."

"I wish he would leave the valley with that money," James said. "But never mind. In just a few more days the railroad is going to default on its land, and we'll get control. Then we'll have the law on our side."

"What if the railroad doesn't default?" Nora asked. "What if they begin service?"

James laughed. "In three more days? There hasn't been a train through here in six months, so there isn't likely to be one through in three days."

"But what if there is?"

James sighed. "I hear there's a guy named Flannigan in charge now. I also hear he's an incompetent fool who thinks he can do singlehandedly what an entire corporation couldn't do. He'll make some puny effort, then he'll give up and the land will be available. In fact, I wouldn't be surprised if Flannigan hasn't already given up."

"If I know Patrick Flannigan, you shouldn't count him out yet," Nora said.

"If you know Pat Flannigan?" James said, surprised by her statement. "What do you mean? Do you know him?"

"No, not really," Nora said quickly. "I did meet him, quite by accident, on the way out here."

"Evidently he made quite an impression on you," James said. "At least, enough of an impression to lead you to think he may succeed."

"I have nothing to base that on," Nora said. "He just impressed me as a most aggressive young man, that's all."

James chuckled. "It will take more than aggressiveness to save this railroad," he said. "It will take money. It will take a great deal of money, and I know that Mr. Flannigan is in short supply of that particular commodity. But, enough of that, did you enjoy the evening?"

"Yes," Nora answered.

"I hope you will allow me to provide you with many more such evenings," James said.

CHAPTER SIX

The next morning the parishioners of St. Martin's Episcopal Church were out front, visiting after church, when they were interrupted by the sound of a train whistle. For just a moment everyone looked at each other in surprise, for there had been no train through Jordan Valley for nearly four months.

"It's a train," Mr. Fisher, the banker, said, as if everyone didn't know. Somehow, putting it in words seemed to galvanize the others to action.

"A train!" someone else yelled, and the call was passed on, so that within a minute not only the parishioners of St. Martin's, but the congregations of the Baptist and Methodist churches, as well as those who hadn't gone to church at all, knew that a train was coming to Jordan Valley.

Everyone began moving toward the depot, slowly and hesitantly at first, as if unsure of themselves. Then, as the train grew closer, they could hear the venting of steam and the puff of smoke. The long, lonesome sounding whistle blew again, and its sound hurried the people on. Soon, the townspeople were gathered on the platform of the boarded-up depot.

"Here she comes," someone called, though his shout was hardly necessary, for everyone watched as the train came around the curve and into the town itself. It was pulling a string of empty cars. Already some of the children were running alongside, shouting, and jumping with glee.

"My, have you ever seen anything so beautiful?" Sterling asked, as the train drew up alongside the station platform.

Nora recognized the green and red brass trimmed engine as the same one she had ridden in going to Boise with Pat Flannigan. Then, leaning out the cab window behind the engineer, she saw the smiling face of Patrick Flannigan.

And something else!

The train rolled to a majestic stop, then squirted steam from the driver wheel cylinder. The great puff of steam first frightened, then amused those who were too close when they realized there was no danger. Pat climbed down from the engine, where he was immediately surrounded by the citizens of the town.

"Who are you?" someone shouted.

"I'm Pat Flannigan, president of the Valley Spur Railroad line," Pat answered.

"Have we got train service now?"

"You see her sitting here, don't you?" Pat answered with a broad grin.

"Can I buy a ticket now?"

"What about the grant land? Does it belong to you now?"

Pat laughed and held up his hands, begging for some quiet.

"Ladies and gentlemen, I am going to hold a town meeting this afternoon, right here in this depot," he said. He looked toward it. "As soon as I can get it clean enough for people to go in."

The people laughed.

"What's the meeting for?" someone asked.

"It's to answer any questions that any of you may have concerning the Valley Spur line," Pat said.

"What time?"

"Two-thirty," Pat said. He smiled. "Provided you quit asking me questions now so I can get to work."

Reluctantly, the crowd began to break up, then drifted away, talking among themselves as they speculated about the possibility of railroad service being restored.

"Pat, I'm going to vent all the steam and bank the fire," the engineer called down from the cab.

"All right, Sollie. Then you, Emmett, and Ira come and help me with the depot."

"Right," Sollie replied.

Pat looked at the engine proudly, then he wiped away an imaginary spot from the shining green paint with his handkerchief.

"I am Professor Sterling Cassidy, sir," a voice said from behind him, and Pat turned quickly toward him. The professor was not quite as tall as Pat, though he was a good-sized man, and handsome enough that Pat saw easily why Nora was so pretty.

Pat stuck out his hand. "I'm very glad to meet you, sir. I'm Pat Flannigan."

"Would you mind explaining this?" Professor Cassidy asked, pointing to the name on the engine cab.

"Isn't she beautiful, though?" Pat asked. "She's a 4-4-2, tall, wide and handsome. And look at the size of the driver wheels."

"I don't mean the engine, sir, I mean the name," Sterling said. "My daughter seemed quite upset when she saw it, and I am most concerned."

"Nora was upset?" Pat asked. "Professor, I'm sorry. I had no idea she would be upset. I certainly wouldn't have done it, had I known that."

"Why did you do it? And how do you know her? I had no idea the two of you had ever met."

Pat laughed, a small, friendly laugh.

"I really don't know her, Professor," he said. "I did meet her briefly, and I was struck with her beauty. Then, when it came time to name the engine, I wanted a name worthy of such a beautiful engine, and the beauty of your daughter came to mind. So, I named it the Nora Cassidy Special. Where is Nora? Perhaps if I talked to her."

"No," Sterling said. "Let me talk to her first. If she's willing to talk to you, I'll send her over to the depot."

"Thank you," Pat said.

Sterling looked at the engine and the long line of cars. "And now, Mr. Flannigan, I want to ask you a few questions, not as a father, but as a newspaperman. Are you serious about restoring rail service to the valley?"

"Yes," Pat said.

"You sound awfully sure of yourself," Sterling said. "While I am inordinately proud of this valley, I am the first to admit that the economics don't justify rail service. Except for a few shipments of cattle during the shipping season, what will be your customer base? Surely you don't expect to make it on passenger service?"

"No," Pat said. "I have another plan."

"Another plan?"

"Yes," Pat said. "But it isn't one I care to discuss yet. I must first establish rail service before this plan has any chance of succeeding."

Sterling smiled. "Would I be missing my guess if I

suggested that you would have to establish rail service before the 30th?"

"You are an astute man," Pat said.

"Then it does have something to do with the grant lands?"

"Yes," Pat said.

"Mr. Flannigan, it is no secret that you have been given a loan by the Great Western Bank. It is also no secret that they only advanced you ten-thousand dollars. That hardly seems enough money to run a railroad."

Pat smiled and pointed to the three men who were working in the depot.

"Do you see those three men?" he asked. "Sollie is the railroad engineer, Emmett, his fireman, and Ira, his brakeman and conductor. They are the only three men I have on the payroll. I have no other encumbrances, other than the service debt owed to the Great Western. Ten-thousand dollars *is* enough, as soon as I start bringing some money in."

"Well, Mr. Flannigan," Sterling said. "I wish you every success on what seems to me an impossible venture. I must say we have sorely missed rail service here, and I am certain that everyone wishes you only the best."

"Good," Pat said. "I hope the people here, and the railroad, prosper mutually. By the way, you will speak with Nora, won't you? I'd like very much to talk to her."

"I'll speak with her," Sterling promised.

Sterling didn't find Nora at the house, so he walked down to the newspaper office. There he found her arranging type. Sterling knew it was just busy work.

Sterling took off his hat and hung it on the hat rack. He rubbed his hand through his hair and looked at his daughter. She was pretending great concentration upon her task.

"Mr. Flannigan says that rail service will be restored by tomorrow."

"I'm certain that is news which will be well received," Nora replied.

Sterling looked at his daughter, at the quick, nervous movements of her hands, and the set expression in her face. He waited, hoping she would volunteer some information, but she remained silent. Finally, Sterling himself broke the silence.

"He calls you Nora."

No answer.

"He speaks as if he knows you, Ra. He says he wants to talk to you."

"I don't want to talk to him," Nora replied. She dropped a letter, and Sterling bent down to pick it up.

"Here," he said. He put his hand over her hand as he gave her the type set letter, and that stopped her work. She stood there for a moment, without looking at him.

"How do you know him?"

Sterling's question surprised Nora. She had told him she came home to help with the paper, and he had expressed such pleasure over seeing her again that he never questioned her about it.

"I rode in the engine with him, that's how I know him," Nora said.

"You rode in the engine with him?"

"That was all there was, there were no cars attached. He offered to take me to Boise; otherwise, I would have had a very long stagecoach ride."

"Evidently, you made quite an impression on him," Sterling said.

James was sitting on the leather settee in the parlor of his house. He was fingering a rawhide quirt as he listened to Buck Andrews. Several other ranch owners were also there, having come naturally to James's house as they heard of the arrival of the railroad.

"The way I look at it," Buck was saying, "this fella Flannigan has got to have it in mind to sell us the land. I figure he's countin' on usin' it as a means of raisin' money to operate."

"That makes sense to me," one of the others said. "What do you think, James?"

"What you gentlemen are saying makes sense," James said, "but the question is, what price is Mr. Flannigan aiming to put on the land?"

"Well, whatever price he sets, he's pretty well got us over a barrel, doesn't he?" one of the ranchers suggested. "I mean, we need that land. There's not a one of us here who isn't runnin' more cattle than our own land can support."

"Perhaps so," James replied, "but does it seem fair to you gentlemen to have to pay an exorbitant rate for that which should rightfully be ours in the first place?"

"What do you mean?"

"Tell them, Buck."

"What James is talking about is the fact that his Papa and me could have filed on that land years ago, back when we first come here. We didn't neither one of us file on it, thinkin' at the time that it would be greedy to take more'n we could use. Besides, keepin' it open land sort of made it ever'body's land."

"Yeah, that was sort of how I looked at it too," one of the other, older ranchers said. "I didn't come here 'til after you 'n' Louis Wilson had already settled, but I seen what you done with the range land and I did the same thing."

"It would have belonged to all of us, just as it was intended," James said. "Except for one problem. The government decided to use that land as incentive to get the railroad in here. Without consulting with us, they took claim to the land, and made a conditional grant to the railroad."

"Maybe this here Flannigan fella won't meet the conditions," someone put in.

"All he has to do is start running the Nora Cassidy Special up and down that track, and he's met that condition," someone said.

"What?" James asked, looking up quickly. "What did you say?"

"I said all he has to do is run his train up and down the—"

"No, no, you said something about Nora Cassidy."

"I'm sorry, James," the rancher said, when he saw how the information affected him. "I thought you knew that Flannigan had named his train the Nora Cassidy Special."

"No," James said. "She *said* she knew him," he added, almost as if speaking to himself. Then when he saw the others looking at him, he grinned sheepishly. "Never mind," he said. "I was just recalling something the lady said. But you are right, Cleve. All Flannigan has to do to meet the conditions is start running his train. So, we can assume that the land is his. Now, we must come up with a plan to buy it, but at a rate *we* consider fair."

"What would you say a fair rate might be?" Buck asked.

"There's one-hundred-thousand acres," James said. "Fifty cents an acre would be fifty-thousand dollars. I would think that would be a lot of money to a man who is desperately in need of it. In fact, it's a lot of money for us to raise, but we can do it."

"You speak as if coming up with that much money is a cinch," Cleve said. "It ain't that easy for me."

"Sure, it is," James said, smiling broadly. "Any bank in the land would lend one dollar on the acre."

"I don't understand," one of the others said. "If *we* could get a dollar on the acre, why couldn't Flannigan?"

"Because he's already overextended with his railroad," James said. "He would not be considered a good credit risk."

"You think he would be desperate enough to sell it to us for *half* its mortgage value?" Buck asked.

"Why not?" James replied. "He got it for nothing. And, like we already said, by rights it belongs to us anyway. I figure we're doing him a favor by paying him fifty-thousand dollars."

"All right, James, I'll go along with you," one of the ranchers said. "And maybe all these other folks will too. But what about Flannigan? Maybe he did get it for nothing. He can't be no fool. He has to know the real value of the land. What if he won't sell it to us?"

James got up from the chair and walked over to the roll top desk. He pulled an envelope from one of the pigeon-holes.

"I got a letter from Washington, answering an inquiry I made about the Railroad Grants Act which gave the land to the Valley Spur. There's an interesting paragraph here I'd like to read to you."

James cleared his throat and began to read: "...Therefore, in order to take possession of the land known as the Jordan Valley Railroad Grant land, the Valley Spur line must begin operation on, or before, June 30th, 1881, and they must sustain that operation on a scheduled basis for at least six months."

James put the letter back in the envelope and looked at the others with a smile on his lips.

"So, what does that mean?" Cleve asked. "He's going to start his service tomorrow."

"He must sustain regularly scheduled service for six months," James said. "Now I ask you, gentlemen. If we don't give him our business, how is he going to continue his operation?"

Cleve smiled broadly. "Oh," he said. "I think I'm beginnin' to get the picture here. What you're sayin' is we'll tell the fella to sell us the land at our price...or he gets no business from us. Is that it?"

"That's it exactly," James said. "We'll organize a total boycott of his operation. He can only run his train up and down those tracks empty for so long, then he's going to have to do one of two things. He's either going to have to come to terms with us, or he's going to go out of business. In other words, gentlemen, we have just jerked a cinch into him."

Cleve laughed. "You know, James, you are a sneaky son-of-a-bitch. I'm sure glad we're on the same side."

CHAPTER SEVEN

Nora stood on the depot platform and looked up at the engine. Even cold and silent, it seemed alive to her, and she recalled that thrilling afternoon she had ridden in the cab from Twin Falls to Boise. And now this beautiful engine had her name. She had reacted badly when she first saw it, more out of shock than anything else. Now, though she still wouldn't admit it to anyone, she felt a sense of pride because of the distinction.

"Nora!" a voice called from the door of the depot. "Nora, you *did* come!"

"So," Nora said, as Pat approached her, "I see you've made good your promise to start rail service."

"Yes," Pat said. The smile left his face and he looked at Nora seriously for a moment. "Your father told me you were displeased at seeing your name on the engine. I meant no disrespect at all. If you wish, I'll remove your name."

"Why bother?" Nora said. "Everyone has seen it now. The damage has been done."

Pat smiled brightly. "You mean I can keep it on?"

"You may as well," Nora replied.

"I'll tell my engineer that you've agreed to it."

"What? You mean you won't be the engineer?" Nora asked, with a teasing grin.

"You've a serpent's tongue about you, girl, for recallin' my difficulty with the beast. Come on, look over the depot…perhaps it could use a woman's touch. You might give me an idea as to how to make it a bit more attractive."

Nora followed Pat into the building, which had been boarded up for some time. Three men were working inside, sweeping the floor, picking up trash, and washing windows. Despite their efforts the building still had a dank, unattractive look and smell.

"The best thing you could do is tear it down and start all over," Nora said, wrinkling her nose in distaste.

"I'm inclined to agree with you," Pat said, looking around in despair. The partition around the ticket window was half tom down. "Unfortunately, this is the only thing we have, so we have to use it."

"Hey, Pat, I found the clock back there," Ira said. "And it still works. I just set it."

"Put it on the wall," Pat said. "We can't have a time schedule if we don't have a timepiece. Is that the right time?"

"Yep, five of two," Ira said, as he set the clock on a small shelf that protruded from the wall.

"The town meeting is scheduled in here at two-thirty," Pat said.

"Two-thirty?" Nora gasped. "You mean you're going to have the entire town in here in a little over thirty minutes?"

"Yes," Pat said.

Nora sighed. "Give me a broom," she said, taking one from Sollie.

"I don't have time to go home and change," Nora said. "And if you're going to have the entire town in here, the least you can do is have the place clean."

"Right," Pat said happily, beaming proudly over the fact that Nora had pitched in to help them. "Oh, say, what about curtains? Do you think they would help?"

"I wouldn't put up curtains," Nora said. "They'd just block out the light, and you should let in as much light as you can. Also, have the man who is cleaning the windows change the water. It's so dirty now that he's doing little more than spreading the dirt around."

"Good idea," Pat said. "Emmett, you heard the lady. Go fetch some clean water."

By two-thirty the people of the town began coming toward the depot in twos, threes, and larger groups. Entire families came, many even with babes in arms, and they looked around curiously, sensing the excitement of the meeting. The older children ran around the train, looking up at it in open-mouthed wonder, ignoring the calls of their mothers to come away before they got run over.

The depot was clean, though some of the more obviously damaged areas still stood in need of repair. Pat stood just in front of the ticket window, watching as the men and women came inside and settled on the benches of the waiting room. Finally, the people stopped coming, and Pat assumed they were all present, so he started to talk.

"Folks, my name is Pat Flannigan," he said. "I intend to set up an office right here in this building, and in that office, I will conduct all the business of the Valley Spur line. If any of you merchants, or ranchers, or anyone else, for that matter, have any freight shipments you want to arrange, I can take care of them."

"What about passenger service?" one man asked.

"Yes, sir," Pat said. "In fact, with the establishment of this service, it is now possible for a person to step on the train here at noon on Monday, and eat your noon meal in

New York City, the following Sunday."

"Mister, do you know what you're saying? It took me nine months to get out here," someone said, and everyone else laughed.

"Did you come by wagon?"

"Sure did. Left from Saint Louis."

"I imagine you made about ten miles per day on the trip out," Pat said. "It might interest you to know that on this train, you can go further in *one hour* than it was possible to go in an entire week by wagon."

There were gasps and exclamations of wonder at the news.

"Yeah, but does this here train go all the way to New York?"

"No," Pat admitted. "It goes to Boise, Idaho. There, you can make connections to take you anywhere in the country."

"Is it safe?"

As that question was asked, the train whistle was blown, and Pat smiled.

"Ah, that's the signal that the engineer has the steam built back up. And now, sir, to answer your question as to whether it is safe or not, I'm going to demonstrate. If you would all step outside, please, Ira Hayes, our conductor, will help you board the train. I'm providing a free train ride for everyone."

At that announcement, the children, who had been paying attention to what was going on, let out a loud cheer. Some of the men also cheered, though reaction from most of the women seemed to be one of apprehension.

"How far are we goin'?" one of the men wanted to know.

"Just up to Boise Pass," Pat said. "As you know, the view from up there is quite beautiful."

"What do you mean, *just* up to the pass? Mister, that's thirty miles from here."

"We'll be there in less than an hour," Pat promised. "In fact, I'll have you back here before six o'clock this evening, in time for dinner."

"You mean supper, don't you? Most of us has done et dinner."

Pat smiled. "Yes, I meant supper. Now, who wants to go?"

"Me, me!" some of the children shouted, and they were through the doors and headed for the train before their nervous mothers could react.

"It's perfectly safe, believe me," Pat assured everyone.

Gradually people began to move toward the train, so that by the time the steam valve was open and the train moving, nearly half of the town had taken Pat's offer.

Nora stood in the door of the depot and waved to many of the passengers as the train began backing away. Only the engine was actually backing, having been disconnected, and then shunted around a switch to the opposite end of the train.

"Is he going to back all the way to the pass?" Nora asked Pat, who had stayed behind.

"Yes," Pat said. "A steam engine is just as efficient backing as it is going forward. Once up there, he can shunt around to the front of the train again. We have to do that because we don't have a roundhouse where the engine can be turned around. Why didn't you go?"

Nora smiled. "I just had a week on a train, remember? Come, I want you to meet someone."

"Who?"

"James Wilson," Nora said.

"I've heard the name," Pat said. "He's a rancher, isn't

he?"

"Yes."

"James, this is Patrick Flannigan," Nora said when she got the two men together.

"Glad to meet you, James," Pat said, sticking his hand out.

James looked at Pat's hand for just a moment, then took it, but only perfunctorily.

"Flannigan, let's get right down to business," James said. "I'm going to have a meeting out at my ranch tomorrow night. I'd like you to be there."

"Will the other cattlemen be there as well?" Pat asked.

"Every cowman in the county," James said.

Pat smiled. "Then I'll be there. I think we have a little business to discuss."

Though James's meeting was billed as a ranchers' business meeting, any occasion for a large gathering of people was as much a social event as business. For that reason, the ranchers' wives and many of their children came to James's ranch that evening. They dressed up, and arrived in phaetons, broughams, landaulets, and other elegant carriages, though there were also a sprinkling of the more pedestrian conveyances, such as buggies, buckboards, and wagons.

"I've laid the table," Mattie Andrews said, coming up to stand beside James and look out over the crowd of people who had gathered at his invitation. "I dare any of these galoots to leave the meeting hungry."

James looked at Mattie and smiled. "Mattie, if you set a table as well as you rope and brand, then I'll allow as how the ranchers will eat well tonight."

Buck, who had come up right behind his daughter, laughed at James's comment.

James and Buck watched Mattie as she moved through the crowd of people who had gathered in James's house.

"I wish she would take an interest in men," Buck said. "I'm not going to live forever, and it would be nice to know that she has someone to look out for her."

James laughed. "It seems to me, Mr. Andrews, that Mattie is one girl who will never need looking out for. She's as capable as any man I've ever known. She can ride faster, rope better, brand more surely—in fact, there's very little she can't do."

"Yes, I know," Buck said. "Everyone knows about that, and they speak of that as if it were all there was to the girl. But look at her, James. Just take a good look at her. I'm not blind. I know she's my daughter, but, by thunder, she's a pretty girl too, isn't she?"

Mattie finished her conversation with Mrs. Doran, moved on to speak with a few other guests, then stepped outside, on the front porch.

Nora and her father were arriving at that moment. Their vehicle was a closed wagon with the *Jordan Valley Monitor* logo painted on its side. It lacked the style and elegance of the other carriages, but the closed wooden body allowed them to transport papers in the worst weather and Ensure their dryness.

"I hope they haven't started their discussions yet," Sterling said as he parked the wagon. "If only I hadn't dropped that plate just before we were to print the Emporium handbills."

"Don't worry, Papa. Even if Pat has arrived, the business hasn't begun yet, I'm sure. You know how this type of thing is. The people will visit and socialize for a long time before the business begins."

As Nora and her father reached the porch, they saw Mattie Andrews. She was leaning on the porch rail, looking out toward the tall fir trees on the opposite bank of the Owyhee River, a swiftly flowing stream that cut through the middle of the valley, supplying water year-round and making the valley ideal for cattle ranching.

"Hi, Mattie, what are you doing out here?" Nora asked. "Did it get too loud inside?"

"The action hasn't started yet," Mattie said. "Mr. Flannigan hasn't arrived. I just wanted to come outside and get a little fresh air."

"It is nice out here," Nora agreed.

"Come on, Ra, let's get inside," Sterling insisted. "We're late as it is."

Nora smiled at Mattie, then followed her father into the house. The inside of the house glowed golden with the light of many candles and lanterns, and with the brilliance of the overhead chandelier. Even the gaily colored dresses of the women seemed to add to the brightness.

Nora saw James coming toward them.

"I was getting worried," James said. "I was beginning to think that you might not come. It's going to be a very important meeting, and I think you should be here."

"I wouldn't have missed it for the world," Sterling said. "It's my fault we're late. Just as we were ready to print some handbills, I dropped the plate and scattered type everywhere. We had to reset the entire thing."

"Are you hungry?" James asked. "There's enough food to feed an army laid out on the dining room table."

"James, my boy, you do things grandly, don't you?" Sterling said. "I must confess that food sounds very good to me right now, as we had to work through dinner. Ra, won't you join me?"

"Not just now, Papa," Nora said. "I'll get something later. First I want to visit."

"Of all God's creatures, only the human female would rather visit than eat," Sterling said, as he started toward the dining room.

CHAPTER EIGHT

The James Wilson ranch was as easy to find as Pat had been told it would be. It was a huge house with cupolas, dormers, arches, scrollwork, and wrought iron adornment, and Pat had the rather ungracious thought that it looked more like a wedding cake than a house. On this particular night it was well lighted, with a glow of gold spilling from every window. It was surrounded by horses and carriages.

As Pat tied his horse to the hitching rail, he could hear the river rushing behind him. He looked around to take in the ranch, not only the main house, but the bunkhouses, barns, horse lots, and the rest. This was an exceptionally well maintained and affluent looking ranch. It appeared as if Mr. James Wilson had everything a man could want: money, position, a fine house and a large ranch.

Pat walked up onto the porch and pulled the bell cord. The door was opened almost immediately by a very pretty woman with soft brown hair and flashing blue eyes. She laughed.

"Well, now, I *know* you must be Mr. Flannigan," she said. "I know everyone else." She stuck out her hand. "I'm Mattie Andrews."

"You're right about me," Pat replied, smiling at her friendliness. "I am Pat Flannigan."

"You don't look like a monster, Mr. Flannigan, despite what they're all saying," Mattie said.

"Oh? Am I supposed to be some kind of a monster?"

"To some, you are."

"Why? Doesn't the valley want rail service?"

"Oh, we want rail service all right," Mattie said. "But we also want the grazing land."

"I see," Pat said. "By grazing land, you're talking about the railroad grant land, are you not?"

"Yes," Mattie said. "They're in the library right now, trying to come up with a plan to keep the land."

"Why aren't you in there?" Pat asked. "Aren't you interested in what happens to the graze land?"

"I'm a woman," Mattie said.

"I noticed," Pat smiled. "I may not look like a monster, but you *do* look like a woman."

"I accept that as a compliment," Mattie said. "And I appreciate the thought. But the truth is, I'd much rather be in there with the men than in the parlor with the other women, carrying on all their foolish pratter-waller. I'm as good a rancher as any man in there, and I've got a right to know what's going on, seeing as it might affect my ranch."

Pat followed Mattie down a wide hall toward the library. The hallway was furnished with a couple of hall stands, a table, and a large grandfather's clock. The walls were hung with antler racks, Indian carpets, and a rather large painting of a stern looking man in a heavy beard. A brass plate beneath the picture identified the man: *Louis W. Wilson:* 1824-1879.

"That's Uncle Louis," Mattie said.

"Uncle? You mean James Wilson is your cousin?"

Mattie laughed. "Not really, but Dad and Uncle Louis settled this valley together, so Mr. Wilson became sort of an honorary uncle. He was a good man. It was a sad day when he died."

The door to the library was open, and as they approached, they could hear someone speaking.

"That's James's voice," Mattie whispered.

"...stick together, the railroad cannot dictate terms to a united group of ranchers. I say that Mr. Flannigan will listen to our terms, or he can listen to the rattle of empty trains."

Pat stepped into the doorway just as the last words were spoken. He leaned against the door without announcing his presence. Mattie stayed just outside and out of sight.

"James, I need to get some cattle to market soon," one of the other ranchers said. "I had a hard winter, and I don't really have enough to make a trail drive practical. If I could ship some head on through to Denver, I could get a good enough price to get me out of a jam. The railroad seems like a good deal to me."

"Oliver, all I'm asking is that you pull your belt in and stick it out. It might get hard, but in the long run, it will guarantee us the grazing land that we need."

"I'm willing to listen to James Wilson," one of the other ranchers said. "After all, he's the biggest and wealthiest rancher in the valley. He must be doing something right."

"I chose the right Papa," James said, and the others laughed at his self-deprecating remark.

"No matter, I say we listen to him too," another put in. "When this fella Flannigan comes, let's just tell him what we want. As far as I am concerned, we can just dictate our terms to him, and he won't have any say in the matter at all."

"And just what *are* those terms?" Pat suddenly asked. His voice startled the others, and they all turned, as one, to see him standing in the door.

"Well, Mr. Flannigan." James said, "I see you made it to our meeting."

"Just in time, it would appear," Pat said. He walked through the room to stand in the front, next to James. He pulled a cheroot from his inside jacket pocket and lit it, cupping his hand around the match, and puffing out clouds of blue smoke before he waved the match out. "Now," he said, "would someone care to tell me just what terms you are talking about?"

"It has to do with the railroad grant land," James said.

"What about it?"

"Well, it's no secret that you need money, Flannigan. And it's no surprise where you're going to try to raise that money. You are going to try to sell the grant lands to us."

"I've considered that possibility," Pat admitted.

"We are willing to pay you fifty cents an acre for the land," James said.

"Fifty cents," one of the other ranchers shouted. "And not one penny more."

"I see," Pat said. "Gentlemen, I am sure you realize that I had the land appraised while I was putting together the financial package that allowed me to begin business with this railroad. The sale value of that land is at least two dollars an acre, and with aggressive marketing, even more. Why, you can borrow one dollar an acre on it. What makes you think I would sell it to you for fifty cents an acre?"

"The way I see it, Flannigan, you don't have any choice," James said triumphantly. "Because if you don't sell to us at our price, we won't be using your railroad."

"Gentlemen, if you would just think about it for a moment, you would realize that you and the railroad have mutual interests. You depend upon a solvent railroad in order to have access to the best markets for your cattle, and the railroad depends upon solvent ranchers in order to have customers for our service. One hand washes the other, so to speak."

"Tell me, Flannigan," James asked. "In this hand washing operation, what did you plan to charge us for the graze land?"

"Nothing," Pat said.

There was a buzz of surprise and curiosity.

"Nothing? What do you mean, nothing?" James asked.

"I didn't intend to sell you the grant lands," Pat said.

"You aren't going to sell to us?" Buck asked. "Then what are you going to do with the land?"

"Nothing," Pat said. "For the time being, I'm willing to let things stay as they are."

"You mean you are going to let the cattlemen continue to run their cows on the grant lands?" Sterling asked.

"Yes," Pat said.

Again, there was a buzz of surprise and excitement.

"I told you," Pat said, when the buzzing died down. "Our coexistence depends upon a mutuality of interest. One hand washes the other. I will allow your cattle to use the grant land, and you will ship your cattle on my railroad. Are we agreed?"

"You have to have our cattle to survive, right?" James asked.

"You are right on that score," Pat said. "I know you were planning on boycotting the railroad, and I have to confess to you that the prospects of a boycott sounded awfully bleak. If you had done it, I would have to try something else."

James laughed derisively. "Mr. Flannigan, just what else could you have done?"

"Well, you know the old saying," Pat said. "If Mohammed can't go to the mountain, then the mountain will come to Mohammed."

"I think you have that just reversed," Sterling chuckled.

"Not in this case," Pat said mysteriously.

"Has your train service started yet?" James asked.

"I started it today," Pat said. "The train went to Boise, empty. There we will pick up ten cases of canned peaches for Miller's Emporium. That is not exactly revenue producing freight, gentlemen, so as you can see, I am dependent upon your cooperation."

"How much will you charge us?" Oliver asked.

"Fifty cents per head, per hundred miles," Pat said. "It will cost you two and a half dollars to get one cow to Boise."

"What's a head bringing in Boise right now?" Cleve asked.

Pat cleared his throat. "I'll be honest with you, gentlemen," he said. "You won't get any more for your cattle in Boise than you would if you drove them up to Portland and sold them there."

"What?" Oliver asked. "What are you saying? Are you telling us we should pay you two dollars and fifty cents a head to ship our cattle to Boise, where we sell them for the same amount of money we can get in Portland? All things considered, we'd *lose* money if we did something that foolish, wouldn't we?"

"It would have been more honest, Flannigan, if you had told us in the first place that you were going to charge us for using the land," Buck said.

"Believe me, I'm not trying to come up with some

hidden charge," Pat said. "But I ask you to consider this. Denver is paying thirty-five dollars a head. You could ship them on to Denver for another two and a half dollars, and you would net thirty dollars a head."

"We would *net* thirty dollars a head?"

"That's right," Pat said.

"That all sounds fair, Flannigan," James said. "But there are a few questions I'd like to ask."

"You go right ahead and ask them," Pat invited.

"Is it possible for us to contract with your railroad for a shipment all the way to Denver?"

"No," Pat replied. "My railroad goes only to Boise. But you can make further arrangements in Boise to take you on to Denver."

"I see," James said. "In other words, we have to switch railroads?"

"Yes."

"Isn't it true, Mr. Flannigan, that during peak shipping times the cattle sometimes have to remain in feeder lots until enough cars are available to ship them on?"

"Yes," Pat agreed. "But that is true only during peak shipping times. This isn't peak shipping times. That's why the prices for your cattle are so elevated."

"The price for keeping them in feeder-lots is also elevated right now, is it not? In fact, it's fifteen cents per animal. A stay of one month could add four and a half dollars to the cost, and there's no telling what the market for our cattle would be if we had a month's delay. The price might drop to twenty dollars a head, and if it does, we've lost money."

"See here, Flannigan," one of the cattlemen sputtered. "Is that right? Could that happen?"

"That is highly unlikely," Pat said.

"Highly unlikely, but it could happen, right?" Buck

asked.

"No," Pat said, as the group of men began to buzz angrily. "No, that isn't right. You would have to have a combination of highly unusual circumstances for that to occur. Most of the time your shipments would go straight on through, with no problem at all."

"I suppose you are ready to guarantee that," James suggested.

"I can't guarantee it," Pat said. "How can I guarantee the business practice of someone else's business? I can only guarantee that your cattle will arrive in Boise."

"Then the risk is ours to take," James said. "Gentlemen, I don't know about the rest of you, but I have no wish to take that risk."

Pat ran his hand through his hair, then he pulled out his gold nugget and fingered it for a moment. Finally, he made up his mind, and he held up his hand to call for quiet.

"All right," he said. "I'll assume the risk."

"To what degree will you assume the risk?" James asked.

"I will pay the feeder-lot costs in Boise, should there be a delay in shipping the cattle on to Denver. But believe me, there really *is* no risk."

James smiled. "Then we should all come out ahead, shouldn't we?"

"Yes," Pat said.

"How many head can you handle?" James asked.

"I could handle five hundred with no difficulty," Pat said.

"All right," James said. "We'll have five hundred head of cattle at the loading pens Thursday morning. I suppose you would like to be paid then?"

"That would be nice," Pat said, thinking of the

twelve-hundred-fifty dollars.

"You'll have the money," James said. "But I shall expect your signature on a contract in which you agree to the feeder-lot charges, should any occur."

"I'll sign," Pat agreed.

"Flannigan, we have a deal."

"Yahoo!" one of the cattlemen shouted, and the meeting then dissolved into groups of excited ranchers, discussing the unexpected but beneficial outcome of the meeting.

"A net of *thirty* dollars! Hot damn that sounds good!"

"And we're going to keep the range land without having to buy it!"

"Yeah, but what about the squatters?"

"We've handled them up to now, we'll keep on handling them."

CHAPTER NINE

When the roosters crowed on Thursday morning, the sun, its disc blood red and not yet painful to the eyes, turned the Owyhee River into a flowing stream of red.

"It's a handbill," Sterling said. "I received it in the mail yesterday, along with a letter asking me to verify that the claims of the handbill are accurate."

Nora removed the handbill and opened it up, then gasped as she saw its contents.

The best VALLEY FARMING LANDS
are for sale by VALLEY SPUR
RAILROAD LINE

Buy tickets to Jordan Valley, Oregon, and the ticket cost will be applied to the purchase of the land. This is the best farming land in the world. It is available for settlers at only three dollars per acre, and your first year's crop will more than pay for the land. The land may be purchased over a ten-year period, with only a small down payment.

*HALF FARE to Families of Purchasers.
LOW FREIGHT FARE on Household
Goods and Farm Stock.
   Contact Pat Flannigan, Valley Spur
Line, Jordan Valley, Oregon.*

"But I thought he was going to let the cattlemen use the range land," Nora said.

"If you will recall," Sterling said, "Mr. Flannigan's exact words were," Sterling opened Nora's note tablet and read, "'For the time being, I am willing to let things stay as they are.' In fact, as I recall, he even asked you if you were getting it all down."

"Yes," Nora said. "I do recall now. Why, that, that *liar,*" she said.

"He didn't exactly lie," Sterling said. "He just didn't tell us the whole truth. For the time being, he is willing to let things stay as they are, but with the arrival of the first settlers, things will begin to change."

"Are you going to tell James?" Nora asked.

"Honey, I'm going to tell the entire valley," Sterling replied. "I'm running this handbill on the front page of today's paper. Now, do you still want to go over to the Morning Star Hotel and speak with your Mr. Flannigan?"

"Yes," Nora said. "Now more than ever."

Nora walked down the boardwalk toward the hotel. It was just two days until the big Fourth of July celebration, and already a banner was strung across the street. It swung gently in the morning breeze, and the sign in front of Dr. Conkling's Apothecary, to which the banner was attached, made a squeaking sound as she walked by. The banner read, *"Jordan Valley wishes Happy Birthday to the U.S.A., July 4th, 1881"* Nora nodded politely to half a dozen greetings, then stepped into the lobby of the Morning Star Hotel.

The desk clerk looked up and smiled as Nora entered.

"Good morning, Miss Cassidy. You haven't come for the advertising copy, have you? Your father picked that up two days ago."

"No, nothing like that, Mr. Peterson. I've come as a reporter, not an ad salesman. Which room is Mr. Flannigan's?"

"Mr. Flannigan is in room 208," Peterson said, without having to check the register.

"I'll just go on up, if you don't mind," Nora said, starting for the wide, carpeted staircase.

Room 208 was at the far end of the hall. She walked down the red-carpeted hallway until she stood just outside the door. She knocked, waited for a few seconds, then knocked again.

"Mr. Flannigan?"

"Just a minute," a muffled voice answered.

Nora stood there quietly until the door opened. Pat saw her, then he smiled broadly and pulled the door all the way open.

"Come in," he said. "Come on in. What a pleasant surprise."

"Yes," Nora said. "We both seem to be in the business of providing surprises, don't we? Only some of the surprises aren't so pleasant."

The smile left Pat's face, and he looked at Nora with a confused expression.

"What do you mean?" he asked. "What are you talking about?"

"I'm talking about the best farming land in the world," Nora said. "For sale, cheap, by the Valley Spur Railroad."

"Where did you hear about that?" Pat asked.

"There is no need for you to deny it, Mr. Flannigan. I saw one of the handbills you have distributed. I must say that we could have done a better printing job, but the information is quite legible. Certainly, legible enough to bring hundreds of settlers into this valley."

"I see," Pat said, quietly. "And you wouldn't want that to happen?"

"Mr. Flannigan, this is a ranching valley," Nora said. "Our economy is based upon cattle. Without the range land the cattle ranchers will suffer, and when they suffer, the entire economy of the valley will suffer."

"That's where you're wrong," Pat said. "The best thing that could happen to this valley would be to diversify the economic base. Don't you see? If a few hundred more people come into the valley and began raising crops, their income would benefit everyone. The merchants would get their business, I would get their business, even the newspaper would have more readers and more advertising."

"And the ranchers?"

"They won't suffer," Pat said. "Perhaps they won't have the same stranglehold on the valley they have now, but they won't suffer."

"I...I wish I could believe you, Pat," Nora said, and her words were spoken with an intensity that surprised Pat. It also did not escape his notice that she called him Pat. "We need to talk," she said. "Not only about this, but about a few other things as well."

"Nora, I'd be only too happy to talk to you, for I'm sure I could make you see my side of it." Pat stepped back and held his arm out, inviting her into his room. "Come on in."

Pat saw the discomfort Nora felt over entering the room, so he added, "Or perhaps you'd feel more comfortable in the restaurant. I haven't had my breakfast. Would you like to join me?"

"I've had breakfast, thank you," Nora said. "But we could talk as you eat, if you don't mind." She would be safe in the dining room, she knew.

"I don't mind at all," Pat said. "Come along."

Just as Pat started to pull the door to, a woman called from the end of the hall at the top of the stairs.

"Pat, wait! I left something in your room this morning, and I want—"The woman saw Nora and she stopped. "Oh," she stammered. "Excuse me, Pat, I didn't realize you had company."

Nora looked at the woman. She was very pretty, though in a showy sort of way. Her hair was brown, and her eyes were blue, but the most striking thing about her was her rouge. Nora had never seen that much rouge on a woman, especially at this hour of the morning. The woman also reeked of perfume.

"It's all right, Rosie," Pat said. "The room is unlocked. Go on in and look around."

"Thanks," Rosie said. She passed by with her eyes looking down toward the carpet

"Do you know Mrs. Mullens?" Nora asked.

"Do you?" Pat replied.

"Only by name, I'm afraid," Nora said. "I have never figured out exactly what it is she does. I know she works here at the hotel, perhaps as head housekeeper or something."

Pat chuckled. "Or something," he said.

"She called you by your first name."

"We've grown rather close," Pat suggested with a wry smile.

"Close? What do you mean, close?" Nora asked.

"Rosie and I spent the night together," Pat said.

Nora gasped.

"I'm sorry," Pat said. "I thought you realized that Mrs. Mullens was a prostitute."

"I realized no such thing," Nora said. "How *could* I know that? How would any *decent* person know that?"

"Oh, I see," Pat said. "And of course, being a decent person, you are totally blind to life all around you."

"I try and avoid coming in contact with the seamier aspects of life, yes," Nora said. "And so should you."

"And so should I?" Pat said, raising his voice. "'N' would you be for tellin' me, lassie, who gave you the callin' to tell me how to live my own life, now?" Pat's Irish brogue, intensified, with the increase of his Irish temper.

"Oh," Nora said. "Oh, I should have my head examined for coming over here. To give you a chance to explain about the land."

"And so I did explain about the land," Pat said.

"And the woman you spent the night with," Nora said. "Can you explain her?"

"Now, wait a minute," Pat said. "What right do you have to tell me that any explanation is due?"

"You are quite correct, sir, I have no right," Nora said angrily. "But neither do you, sir, have a right to be offensive in my company."

"Madam, I would remind you that you came to my room of your own volition," Pat said coldly. "And you may leave the same way."

Nora looked toward Pat with eyes which were snapping with the light of anger.

"Thank you for giving me your permission to withdraw," she said. "For that is exactly what I shall do."

Nora turned sharply on her heel and walked quickly and haughtily down the corridor, leaving Pat to stare at her as she walked away.

"I'm sorry, Pat," Rosie said, returning from Pat's room at that moment. "I had no idea she would be up here, or I would have waited."

"Ah, don't worry about it, Rosie," Pat said easily. "It doesn't mean anything."

"You name your train after her, and you say it doesn't *mean* anything?"

"Rosie, m'girl, you do have a point," Pat said, laughing at her comment, "How'd you like to eat breakfast with me?"

"Sure," Rosie answered. "I'll get breakfast sent up and we can—"

"No, I mean in the dining room," Pat said.

Rosie looked shocked. "You would eat with me, in public?"

"Of course."

"You wouldn't be shamed by my presence?" Rosie asked.

"Sure now, 'n' would you be for tellin' me how an Irish lad could ever be shamed by bein' seen with a colleen as pretty as yourself?" Pat asked, throwing a great deal of brogue into his voice.

"Michael, sure'n I'd consider it a great honor to eat breakfast with you," she said, imitating his brogue.

When Pat went down to the depot after breakfast, he saw that Jordan Valley had started its Independence Day celebration early by making the loading of the train a gala event. In the spirit of the event, Sollie, Emmett, and Ira, had decorated the train in red, white, and blue bunting. The brass had been polished until it shined with blinding brightness. Twenty-five cattle cars, loaded with twenty head each, stretched out behind the engine, making a line from the depot, all the way to the western edge of town.

The cowboys who herded the cattle into the loading pens, were dressed in their best work clothes, and the entire town was turned out to watch. Nora's news had evidently not spread to the others, for no one mentioned the handbill, or the fact that new settlers would be coming into the valley.

Pat climbed up on the first cattle car and looked out over the crowd. Sollie opened the throttle and the train started forward. Pat began walking toward the back of the train, so that in effect he was remaining in the same place with respect to the crowd, though the train was pulling out from under him. When he reached the caboose, he waved back at the crowd. He stayed there until the train was well out of town and starting up the long grade for Boise Pass.

CHAPTER TEN

James Wilson stood in the crowd with the others until the train carrying his cattle disappeared around the far curve of the track. Then, when only a pencil-thin strip of smoke told where the train was, he walked over to the Wells Fargo office, where he checked on the reply to the telegram, he had dispatched the day before.

"Yes, sir, it's back," the operator said. He pulled a yellow envelope from a box and handed it to James.

"Thanks, Tim," James said, as he read the message. He smiled. "This is just what I wanted to hear."

"I was a little surprised you used the Wells Fargo line to send that message," Tim said. "It bein' railroad business, I'm sure Flannigan would've sent the message for free."

"I had my reasons, Tim," James said. "I did have my reasons."

James stuck the message into his pocket, then walked down the boardwalk toward the *Jordan Valley Monitor* office. Sterling and Nora were both busy getting the day's newspaper set.

"I know you have a deadline," James said, "but I was still surprised that you two weren't down at the station, watching the train pull out."

Sterling handed the handbill to James. "What do you think of that?" he asked.

James read Pat's handbill, and then, to the surprise of both Sterling and Nora, he laughed out loud.

"Well, I must say, you are certainly taking this better than I thought you would," Nora said.

"It's wonderful," James said. "It just makes what I did all the sweeter."

"What you did? I don't understand," Nora said. "What did you do?"

"I just made certain arrangements which are going to make it most difficult for Mr. Flannigan to hold onto his land, that's all."

"What do you mean?"

"Oh, nothing," James said, very mysteriously. "Let's just say I purchased some insurance in case something like this should develop. Now I can see that it was a most propitious move on my part."

"I'm glad to see you are taking it so well," Sterling said. "I just hope that Mr. Flannigan takes the Polecat column as well."

"What do you mean?"

"Papa has written a rather blistering editorial against Mr. Flannigan and his underhanded, sneaky tactics," Nora said.

"Good for you, Professor," James said. "And you, Nora, what do you think of the article?"

"I think it is time someone put Mr. Flannigan in his place," Nora replied, with a surprising amount of bitterness.

James smiled broadly and rubbed his hands together. "Well, I'm glad to see you feel that way. And don't worry. Flannigan is going to discover that he bit off more than he can chew when he came to Jordan Valley. I'll see you Saturday," he said, waving goodbye as he walked back outside. He chuckled to himself. He was going to beat Flannigan and it was going to be sweet. Oh, it was going to be sweet.

As the Nora Cassidy Special rolled into Boise, Pat hopped down from the caboose while the train was still rolling and walked across the station platform toward the freight and passenger office. The train continued to move slowly through the station yard toward the feeder-lots, for they would have to off-load the cattle there, then load them onto the cars for transshipment to Denver.

Pat looked over toward the spur tracks, expecting to see the cars he would need. He had wired ahead for them just before he left Jordan Valley. They should have been here by now, unless there was some unexpected delay.

"Howdy, Pat," Eb said, as Pat stepped into the station. Eb was stamping freight manifests.

"Hello, Eb," Pat said.

"I see you brought your cattle."

"Yes," Pat said. "Listen, have you heard anything from the Denver and Missouri? They were supposed to have cars here to take my cattle on."

"I haven't heard a word since you wired me yesterday to order the cars," Eb said. "Would you like me to check on it?"

"Yes, would you? I'm going over to the hotel to take a bath and grab a nap. I'll be back in a couple of hours."

"I should have word by then," Eb promised.

"I'd like to think that the cars will be here by then," Pat said.

"Oh, by the way," Eb said. "Will you be ready to take

some passengers Monday?"

"I've got passengers?"

"I'll say," Eb said, "There are about twenty immigrants wanting to settle your land."

"Really?"

"Yep. Your handbills seem to be doing the job. They've all paid cash for the land, too. I'm holding over six hundred dollars for you."

Pat smiled broadly. "That sounds good," he said. "I'll be ready for them Monday. Oh, you won't forget the telegram?"

"I'll send it right now," Eb said, starting for the instrument.

* * *

"What do you *mean* there are no cars available for shipment to Denver?" Pat asked Eb when he went back to check on his message.

"Here's the wire," Eb said.

"That's the Denver and Missouri. What about the others?" Pat asked.

"I checked with all of them, Pat," Eb said. "The Denver and Missouri, the Northern Pacific, the Union Pacific. There are no cars available for at least two weeks."

Pat crushed the message, then threw it on the floor. That meant he would have to make arrangements to keep the cattle in feeder-lot pens at his own expense. At fifteen cents per day per animal, Pat didn't need a pencil to figure the arithmetic. If he really did have to wait two weeks before he got his cars, he would wind up losing money on the trip.

"Just as a matter of curiosity," Pat said, "do you have any idea who in the hell *needs* that many cars?"

"Let's see," Eb said. "I think one of the messages did

mention it. Yes, here it is...the Wilson Cattle Company."

"The Wilson Cattle Company?" Pat said. He hit his fist in his hand. "Damn, I should have known! It's James Wilson! Well, Wilson, you may have struck the first blow, but I'll get in the last," he swore under his breath.

* * *

At the quilting booth on the Fourth of July, Mrs. Corley Burleson and Mrs. Fran Jackson were finalists in the quilting bee. Mrs. Burleson's entry was Irish Chain, designed and quilted by her in patches of red, white, green, and gold. It was breathtakingly beautiful, but Mrs. Jackson's Jacob's Ladder, done in shades of red from a bright cherry color to a muted wine, was just as beautiful.

The judges were having a very difficult time selecting the winner, and they looked out over the faces of the anxious crowd, composed of supporters of both women, and knew that whichever they selected, they would leave half the people disappointed. The judges were Nora Cassidy and Mattie Andrews.

"What do you think?" Mattie asked.

"I think we should do what a judge would do in a court of law," Nora replied.

"What's that?" Mattie asked with a little laugh.

"We should go into chambers and take it under advisement."

"What's that mean?"

"That means let's get out of here where we can talk it over without everyone hanging on our every word," Nora said, and she pointed to the crowd of people.

"That's a good idea," Mattie said.

The two women excused themselves, telling the onlookers that they wished to discuss the final two quilting entries, and walked over to the gazebo which stood in the center of town. They bought a lemonade apiece, then sat there in the shade of the gazebo, drinking the cool, refreshing liquid while they watched the workers stringing the lanterns for the evening's dance.

"The dance will be held outside tonight," Mattie said.

"Yes," Nora said. "It will be very nice. Are you going?"

"I don't know," Mattie said, sighing. "I really don't enjoy them all that much."

"Why, Mattie Andrews, how can you say such a thing? I saw you last week and you looked as if you were having a wonderful time."

"I don't know," Mattie said. "It seems odd to be racing against all those men in the horse race one minute, then cuddling up to them in a dance the next."

Nora laughed. "You'll never change, Mattie Andrews."

When the two young women returned to the booth, they were besieged by the anxious supporters of die contestants.

"Who won?"

"Have you come to a decision?"

"It's the Irish Chain, right?"

"No, it's the Jacob's Ladder, the Jacob's Ladder," someone else called.

"Ladies," Nora said; then as she looked over the crowd, she saw that there were a few men, including James Wilson, present as well, "and gentlemen, after a careful deliberation, my co-judge and I declare this contest to be a tie between Mrs. Burleson and Mrs. Jackson, and award each of the contestants the ten-dollar first prize."

Everyone cheered and applauded, and even Mrs. Burleson and Mrs. Jackson, long-time competitors in the event, managed to smile and congratulate each other.

"Wait a minute!" Mr. Fisher called. Mr. Fisher was not only the banker, but also a member of the city council. "Where is the extra ten dollars going to come from? It wasn't accounted for in the city budget."

"I'll donate ten dollars to the city," James Wilson said easily. "I agree with Miss Cassidy and Miss Andrews, there is no way to determine which of these two marvelous quilts is more beautiful, and the ladies who worked on them should share equally the fullest benefits of their labor."

"Why, thank you, Mr. Wilson," Fisher said. "Ladies, that is just one more proof, as if such proof was needed, that James Wilson is one of the finest men in the valley. Let's all give him a hand."

The crowd applauded James, and James, holding up his hands modestly, smiled and waved at them as he worked his way through the handshakes and pats on the back until he reached Nora and Mattie.

"That was very nice of you, James," Mattie said. "You are really the hero in their eyes."

"Ah, it was nothing," James said. "Besides, I'm counting on you to win the money back for me. I've bet on you to win."

"Come on," James said to Nora, as Mattie left for the race. "I have a place all picked out for us, down by the corner. We'll get to see them coming down the stretch, and we'll watch them cross the finish line."

"Here they come!" a man on the roof of the Millers' Emporium called. He was looking through binoculars toward the back road.

"Who's in front?"

"Johnny Sweeney is in the lead," the man called down.

"Ed Farmingdale is second, and Morris Goodwin is third."

"Where's Mattie?" someone called up. "Do you see her?"

"No," the man with the binoculars said. "No, I don't even...wait a minute, there she is, back in the pack. She's running about seventh." There was a groan from the crowd, but one of the men called over to James.

"Get your money ready, Wilson. She's going to lose this one."

"There's Sweeney!" someone called. "They've rounded the final stretch."

"Get back! Get back, give 'im room!" someone called. One man ran across the street, carrying a small ribbon with him, then he held up his end so that it made the finish line.

"Look at that!" someone else called. "Who's that on the black horse?"

"It's Mattie Andrews!" another said.

"She's comin' up fast."

"She won't make it. She doesn't have a chance!"

"I don't know, look, she's already third and she's closing on...no, she got 'im. She's runnin' second now and she's chargin' Sweeney!"

"Sweeney works for you, James, can he hold her off?"

"I don't know," James said. "He's a fine rider, perhaps the best I have. But Mattie is awfully good too. Come on, Mattie!"

"Come on, Mattie!" Nora shouted, and soon many others, except for those who, for financial reasons, were against her, also started shouting encouragement.

The horses entered the end of the street, Mattie and Sweeney far out in front of the others. Both riders were bent low over their mounts, but were raised up from the saddles, holding themselves on with their knees. The horses' manes were flying, their nostrils distended, their muscles rippling, and their hooves drumming a thunder in the street.

The horses flashed by just in front of Nora and James, who saw, with a thrill, that Mattie had pulled in front of Sweeney. Mattie's horse flashed across the ribbon, the winner.

James ran to congratulate Mattie, even before Mattie was dismounted. "Mattie, that was a magnificent ride!" James said. "I've never seen anything so exciting!"

"Nora, what do you think?" James called, taking her into the victory circle. "Isn't Mattie the greatest?"

"Yes," Nora said, and she meant it. Mattie was her dearest friend.

CHAPTER ELEVEN

Suddenly, the music and dance were interrupted by the sound of a train whistle, and everyone looked at each other in surprise. The train wasn't supposed to return until late the next afternoon, and yet, here it was on Saturday night. The whistle continued in a series of blasts which made the music inaudible, and several of the celebrating cowboys grew irritated by it.

"Someone needs to go down to the depot and teach that train driver a few manners," Sweeney slurred. Sweeney was drunk, having gone immediately to whiskey to assuage his feelings over losing the race to a woman.

"Listen to that whistle," someone else said. "It doesn't normally sound like that. Do you suppose something's wrong?"

"I'm goin' down there," someone else said, and soon there was a general exodus from the dance floor to the train depot. By now, the train had arrived in town, and everyone could see it, the great yellow lantern wavering in the dark, the steam, like white tendrils of lace, and the sparks in the smoke, whipping up to scatter red stars among the blue.

"Hey!" someone called. "He's brought our cattle back!"

"What? What are you talking about?"

"Look on the train, dammit! Is them our cattle, or not?"

"I'll be damned! What did he do that for?"

The train stopped with a squeal of brakes, and Pat Flannigan jumped down from the engine cab.

"Wilson!" Flannigan called angrily. "Where's Wilson?"

"I'm right here," James said easily, moving forward from the crowd.

"Here are your cattle," Pat said. "And here is your money." He reached into his shirt pocket and took out an envelope, which he handed to James. "Count it, you'll see that it's all here."

"I think there's any need for that," James said.

"I said count it," Pat repeated speaking very quietly in an attempt to control his anger. "From this moment on, Wilson, any dealings between us will have to be open. There is no trust left."

"Obviously," James replied. "Your promise to allow us to continue to use the range land is proof of that."

"Yeah, what about that, Flannigan?" one of the other ranchers said. "Is the article in the *Valley Monitor* true? Are you opening the range land up for immigrants?"

"Yeah? Well, suppose you explain the situation to us right now. Why did you tell us we could use the range land, if you knew you were going to settle it with squatters?" another rancher asked.

"I was honest with you," Pat said. "I told you I had no intention of selling this land to you, and I also told you that you could continue to use it for the time being. It will be some time before the land is all settled."

"You expect us to share the land with the squatters?" someone asked.

"No," Pat said. "I don't intend to let you use any of the

land now. Not since Mr. Wilson's little trick."

"What's he talking about, James?" one of the others asked.

"Yes, James, what trick is that?" Buck asked.

"No trick," James said. "When I discovered that Flannigan intended to double-cross us, I just managed to work a little double cross of my own. I tied up all the cattle cars between Boise and Denver, so Mr. Flannigan couldn't ship out the cattle we sent with him."

"Why did you do that?"

"Simple," James said. "Mr. Flannigan had guaranteed our shipment. If he didn't have any cars, he would have to feed our cattle. If he had to feed our cattle, he would go broke, and if he went broke, the railroad would go out of business, thus causing those lands to be forfeited."

"Ha!" someone laughed. "That was pretty smart! Good thinking, James."

"As you can see, however, Mr. Flannigan has re-neged on his contract. He didn't deliver the cattle, and he didn't hold them for shipment. Instead, he brought them back to us."

"Yes," Pat said. "I brought them back. Now, if you would be so kind as to take your cattle off my train, gen-tlemen, I would appreciate it."

"Flannigan, you aren't going to be so unsporting as to make these cowboys have to work during the dance, are you?" James asked. "I'm not certain they would appreciate that."

"You're damn right I don't appreciate it," Sweeney said. "And I'm going to show you how much I don't appreciate it."

Sweeney knocked Pat down with a sudden and unex-pected blow. As Pat started to get up, Sweeney still had the advantage since he was on his feet, and he clubbed Pat again.

Now the crowd became a part of it, and they started shouting encouragement to Sweeney, screaming at him to finish Pat off.

Sweeney smiled, and drew his fist back for one final, clubbing blow. But he was overconfident, and he took too long, and Pat was able to regain his feet before Sweeney swung. This time Pat avoided the swing, and countered with a short, vicious chop with his left hand.

Sweeney was stunned by the blow, but as Pat started to hit him a second time, he suddenly found himself jumped by half a dozen angry cowboys, anxious to defend Sweeney, and Pat went down under the pummeling.

"Here!" Sterling shouted, moving into the melee. "You men stop this! Stop this at once!"

"All right, that's enough!" James said, and when he called out, the men who had jumped Pat stepped back from him, leaving him sitting on the ground, holding his hand to a split lip.

"I'm sorry, Flannigan," James said. "It seems that a few of the men have had too much to drink. I think you can understand that tonight would not be a good time to unload your train. They'll do it tomorrow, even though tomorrow is Sunday. Is that fair enough?"

Pat pulled a handkerchief from his pocket and dabbed at the blood.

"I suppose it will have to be," he said. "And Wilson?"

"Yes?"

"Get all the cattle off my land. All of them, do you understand? If you don't get them off, I'll get them off, and I promise you, you won't like the way I do it"

"I'm sure you are correct in that statement, Flannigan,"

James said. "For the truth is, I don't like the way you do anything. And now, ladies and gentlemen, I propose that we not let this unpleasant episode spoil our party," James went on. "Let's get back to the dance."

"Yahoo!" one of the cowboys shouted. "We got the whole night ahead of us, boys!"

Gradually the crowd started back toward the dance floor, which had been constructed in the middle of the street. Then the music started, and the dancing resumed. Pat walked over and sat on the station platform in the dark and watched the party from a distance.

Within fifteen minutes, the party was in such full swing again that anyone who was just arriving would have no knowledge of the fact it had ever been interrupted. Then James walked up to the band leader and asked him to call for attention so he could say a few words.

The band played a fanfare, then James stepped up onto their raised platform. He held his hands up to call for quiet, and everyone looked toward him.

"Ladies and gentlemen, this has been quite a day," he said.

Everyone laughed and someone shouted out: "James, you aren't going to make a speech, are you? You know the town's passed an ordinance against Fourth of July oratory!"

More laughter.

Pat's train crew was in no mood to join the Fourth of July celebrations, but they didn't want to stay back in the dark either.

"The Bull's Neck Saloon is open, Pat. What say we go down there and have a few drinks?" Ira invited.

"You guys go on," Pat said. "I really don't feel like drinking now. When I drink in this condition, I just get drunk."

"That's the idea," Ira said.

"No, thank you," Pat said. "You guys go on, get drunk if you want. But remember, we have to go back to Boise tomorrow to pick up our first load of immigrants on Monday."

"We'll be ready to go, Pat," Ira promised.

Pat watched the three men walk toward the saloon, then he went into the depot. The back room of the depot had been converted into a small apartment for his use. At first, he had thought the room would be too remote from the center of town and from people. Now, that remoteness was just what he wanted.

Pat lit a candle and pumped water into a basin. He took off his shirt and prepared to bathe the cuts and bruises on his face and body. That was when he noticed that his lucky nugget was missing. He shrugged nonchalantly. It hadn't brought him much luck lately, anyway.

As the members of St. Martin's passed through the front doors, James Wilson, who had come to church for the first time in longer than Father Crawford could remember, excused himself from Nora and her father, telling them that he needed to get down to the depot to help with unloading the cattle.

When James reached the depot most of the cattle had already been off-loaded from the cars, which had been shunted off onto the spur track. The cowboys were herding the cattle through the center of town and out onto the range land.

"Them cows sure is thirsty," Sweeney said, taking his hat off and wiping the sweat from his brow. "Fact is, I'm awful thirsty myself."

"I don't see how," James said, "after all the liquor you drank last night."

"Ain't that the truth?" Sweeney agreed. "I never have understood why a man got so thirsty on the morning after drinking so much the night before. Here, Benton, let me help you," he called out, as he saw a cowboy struggling to open one of the doors to another cattle car.

James watched the operation for a few minutes longer, then he turned and walked toward the Cassidy house for Sunday dinner. Things seemed to be heading his way, now.

CHAPTER TWELVE

From the Polecat column, July 17th, 1881:

Unwelcome Change

In but two short weeks, the valley has changed. Nearly one hundred families have arrived, placing a burden on the services provided by the valley, staking claims on land without regard to proper procedure, and in some cases, stealing cows, pigs, and chickens from the older, established valley residents.

Mr. Flannigan may have had in mind the guarantee of business for his railroad by bringing in the immigrants, but so far it has had just the opposite effect. The ranchers have quite effectively boycotted his railroad, and the immigrants themselves seem bent upon driving everyone else away.

One has only to visit the depot to see the effects of such unrestricted travel. The air in the depot, and indeed on the train cars, is fetid and unhealthy. Pipes bearing strange smelling tobaccos are lighted, meals of sausage, garlic, sauerkraut, and dried fish are consumed, bodies in strange appearing costumes are unwashed, thus causing decent folk to seek alternate means of transport. Now while I have no argument against the peoples and races of other countries, I can't help but inquire as to why the Germans, Slavics, and Russians feel they can send the most undesirable of their species to our peaceful valley.

"Ra, the ranchers have called an emergency meeting this evening," Sterling said to Nora as he came back into the newspaper office. "I'm going to attend."

"Very well," Nora said. "Is there anything in particular you want me to do?"

"If you would finish setting the ad for Dr. Conkling's curative powders, we'll have all the ads set for next week's issue."

"I'll do it," she said.

Nora read the claims of the ad placed by Dr. Conkling. His powder, made from "Buffalo Tallow", combined with healing herbs and barks, would cure Rheumatism, Sciatica, Pulmonary, Kidney Difficulties, Malaria, Dyspepsia Liver, and all stomach afflictions.

Nora smiled. With so many wonderful cures around, one would think that the world would be free of all illness. How could people be so naive as to believe such wild claims? And yet, how were these wild claims any different from the claims made by Patrick Flannigan? He promised a utopia to the immigrants and rail service to the valley, but the valley couldn't use his rail service, and the immigrants were finding anything but a utopia.

The front door opened, and Nora looked up to see Mr. Flannigan.

Pat had a rolled-up copy of the newspaper in his hand, and he laid it on the counter. "Is your father in?"

"No," Nora said. "Is there something I can do?"

"Not unless you want to take the responsibility for the articles that have been running about me."

"I *do* take that responsibility, Mr. Flannigan," Nora said. "My father is the author of the Polecat column, but we are in accord on his opinions."

"I see," Pat said. He sighed. "Don't you feel you are being a bit unfair?"

"Not at all," Nora said.

"So what you are saying is that James Wilson has bought you and your father."

"No, he has not!" Nora said, slamming the plate down so hard that some of the type popped out onto the floor. "My father has the courage of his convictions, and he writes what he believes."

"What about you?" Pat asked. "Do you have the courage of your convictions?"

"What do you mean?"

"Would you come with me out to the grant lands to meet some of the immigrants?"

"Why should I?"

"Why should you indeed?" Pat asked. "If your mind is already made up, why confuse it with the truth?"

"All right, Mr. Flannigan," Nora said. "I *will* come with you."

"What?" Pat asked, surprised by Nora's statement. "Are you serious?"

"Yes, I'm serious. Why, aren't you? Are you afraid that the *truth,* as you put it, may not be all that different from the way my father perceives things now?"

"I'll go to the livery stable and saddle a horse for you," Pat said. "I'll be back in ten minutes."

"I'll be ready," Nora said. "Come to my house."

They followed the Owyhee River, and as it rushed and splashed beside them a large, brightly colored fish splashed, and Pat laughed.

"Oh, if I had a pole now, we'd have a nice fish dinner."

"You think you could catch him, do you?" Nora teased.

"Do you think I couldn't?"

"It takes a very special skill to catch fish from the Owyhee." '

"I intend to develop that skill," Pat said.

"When?"

"When my work is done."

"We'd all be better off if you would develop that skill now, and leave the work alone," Nora said.

"Who would be better off? The ranchers? James Wilson?"

"Yes," Nora said. "And the residents of the valley."

"Don't forget, the valley has some new residents now. What about them? Would they be better off if I just left? What would happen to them? And what about Johan Forsberg? Until I came along and gave him some legality, he was faced with herds of cows driven through his fields, fences and storage sheds being destroyed..."

"You gave Forsberg legality?" Nora asked.

"Yes," Pat said. "He bought his land from me, why

shouldn't I?"

"But he is nothing more than a common criminal," Nora said. "He came in here and squatted on the land, even *before* you made the offer. How can you justify that now?"

Pat laughed. "What do you think the *cattlemen* were doing, if they weren't squatting?" he asked. "They had no more legal right than Forsberg."

"Just the same, Forsberg has caused so much trouble for the valley," Nora said.

"No more than the valley has caused for him," Pat answered. He looked up at the mountains that walled the valley, and at the rolling land of the valley floor. "It's so wild and so beautiful," he said. "It's a shame to try and hoard all this in a few greedy hands. After all, this is America—a land of opportunity for everyone."

Nora was beginning to regret having come on this journey with Pat. No matter what she said, he seemed to have the correct answer for it. When she was with James, or her father, or Buck Andrews, or the other ranchers, it seemed just and right to want to deny the immigrants entry into the valley. But Pat was making her feel a sense of guilt over it. It was an unwelcome feeling.

They came across a small rise. Then, below them, they saw a very neat-looking house, barn, and live-stock lot. It was much smaller than James's house, but it appeared to be as well cared for, and the front lawn literally burst with brightness as hundreds of flowers bloomed in colorful profusion.

As they approached the house a woman stood up from working in the garden, and she brushed her hair back from her eyes to look at the approaching riders.

"Hello, Mrs. Forsberg!" Pat called, waving his arm.

The woman smiled broadly. "Ah, Pat, what a pleasant

surprise," she said. "You've come at a good time. I'm about to set the table for the noon meal."

"No, we couldn't put you out any," Pat said. "We've just stopped by for a look, and then we'll ride on."

"Nonsense, Johan and Lars will be comin' in from the field just any minute now. They wouldn't hear of you leavin' without takin' a bite with us." Mrs. Forsberg smiled again. "I've made a nice blueberry pie."

"Say no more," Pat said. "I'd be a fool not to stick around for some of your blueberry pie."

"Young lady, if you're bent on trappin' this man, you better let me give you the recipe for my blueberry pie, for I've never known anyone set as much store by it as he does."

"I, uh, thank you for the thought," Nora said, blushing under the woman's mistaken conclusion.

"Mrs. Forsberg, this is Miss Nora Cassidy," Pat said. "Her father is Sterling Cassidy, publisher of the *Valley Monitor*."

"Is that a newspaper?" Mrs. Forsberg asked.

"Yes," Nora said. She and Pat had dismounted, and Pat tied their horses to the hitching rail.

"Well, it's a good thing for a community to have a newspaper," Mrs. Forsberg said. "We don't get to see one out here very often, but I think they are a good thing. Come on in. I see the men comin' in from the field now."

The inside of the house was as cheery as the outside. It was spotlessly clean, with flowers scattered about in brightly colored bottles, which were passing as vases. Muslin curtains at the windows filled with the soft breeze, and the smell of freshly baked pie permeated the air.

"I put it on the windowsill to cool," Mrs. Forsberg said. "I think it's about ready, don't you?" She held it under Pat's nose.

Pat sniffed appreciatively. "Uhmm, uhmm," he said, nodding his head and licking his lips. "Take it away, Mrs. Forsberg, before I lose control of myself and eat it all, right now."

Mrs. Forsberg laughed and set the pie on the shelf above the stove.

"Patrick!" Johan Forsberg said when he came into the house. "Patrick, it's good to see you!"

"Hello, Mr. Forsberg, Lars," Pat said to the father and son.

Nora looked at Johan Forsberg. The last, and only time, she had ever seen him was the night of the dance, when he had come after James with a pitchfork. How large and menacing he was that night, with eyes that flashed with the fires of hell. He was obviously still as large, but now she felt no fear, for he was smiling in genuine friendship as he greeted Pat.

"Mr. Forsberg, Patrick brought a young lady to see us," Mrs. Forsberg said. "I've invited them to eat."

"Fine, fine," Forsberg said. "Any friend of Patrick Flannigan's is certainly a friend of mine, and you are welcome at our table, Miss..."

"Cassidy," Pat said.

"Cassidy?"

"She's the newspaper lady, Pop," Lars said. "She 'n' her pa are the ones been printin' all those stories about the settlers."

"Oh?" Johan said.

"I've brought her out here to have a look," Pat said quickly. "I thought it was about time she saw both sides of the story."

"Yes," Johan said. "That might be a good idea." The

tone of Johan's voice indicated that he didn't have much hope for a change in conditions, no matter what Nora saw of the settlers' side.

"How are things going?" Pat asked.

"We've had two fields destroyed," Johan said.

"And the Wemmers had their barn burned," Lars put in. "And Peter Wemmer was beat up pretty bad, and he had thirty chickens that was stolen."

"Are they still tearing down the fences?"

"Quick as we can get them up," Johan said. "We're having a meeting tonight, all the settlers, and we are going to organize. I don't intend to put up with this much more."

"Organize how?" Pat asked. "Mr. Forsberg, you aren't planning anything like a vigilante committee, are you?"

"That's what I want to do," Lars put in quickly. "And I know half a dozen others who would join me. Peter Wemmer, for one."

"That would be terribly foolish, Lars," Pat said. "No one wins in a range war."

"All we are wanting to do with our organization is provide each other with aid, when such aid is needed," Johan said. "And maybe if we organized, went to the government with one united voice, someone would listen to us."

"We can't go to the government with one voice," Lars said. "Nearly half the immigrants don't even speak English."

"Lars, there is no room in this household for bigotry," Mrs. Forsberg scolded. "Don't forget, this entire country is made up of immigrants. It's a big valley, and there is room for everyone. Now, let us sit to the table. Johan, you return thanks."

The food was a simple but nourishing fare of fried pork chops, boiled potatoes, greens, and cornbread. Pat was obviously at home with them, laughing and talking as if he were a part of the family. Nora felt strangely reflective and spent the entire meal dwelling on something Mrs. Forsberg had said.

"Don't forget," Mrs. Forsberg had said, *"this entire country is made up of immigrants."*

She was right. Nora had read essays in college extolling the virtues of a country made up of immigrants. Perhaps she and her father and the others weren't giving the settlement a chance to work. And perhaps she, with her college education, could learn a lesson from Mrs. Forsberg.

After dinner, the pie was served, and it was every bit as good as Pat had promised it would be. Nora ate it, feeling guilty over the fact that she enjoyed it so. Shortly after the pie was served, Johan and Lars excused themselves, and returned to the fields for the afternoon. Pat and Nora used that as a cue to leave.

"Is Mr. Forsberg quite the monster you had him pictured as?" Pat asked Nora, as they started back.

"I must say that he was much more pleasant this time than he was the last time I saw him."

"Oh? And when was that?"

Nora told about the time Johan Forsberg had come to the dance and started a fight.

"I know about that," Pat said. "He's never forgiven himself for doing that. But you must remember, he was a desperate man, pushed into a corner. Any creature will lash out under such circumstances."

"You like him, don't you?"

"Yes," Pat said. "The Forsbergs are good people. Most of the immigrants are good people if you give them the chance," he added. "I'm sure they aren't all saints, but then what other group of people could make the claim that they were?"

Nora chuckled.

"What is it?"

"Mrs. Forsberg. She called you Pat, yet she calls her own husband Mr. Forsberg."

Pat laughed. "Well, I suppose I just look like a Pat, and he doesn't."

As they rode, the breeze intensified, carrying with it the feel and smell of impending rain. Over the hills, great, billowing clouds darkened, then began to rumble with distant thunder.

"We'd better get a move on," Pat said. He urged his horse into a trot, and Nora's horse kept up with him. They moved at the increased rate for about three or four minutes, but then the rain started.

The rain fell in torrents, drenching them as thoroughly as if they were standing under one of the many mountain cascades.

"Nora, this way," Pat said, turning off the trail.

"What? Where are you going?"

"There's an abandoned house over this way. Come on, it'll get us out of this."

Nora followed him, barely able to see him through the driving rain, until finally a small, weather-beaten cottage loomed dimly in the distance.

"Hurry!" Pat called, urging his horse into a lope. Nora followed, urging her horse on faster, until at last they were there.

The roof of the cottage extended out to one side, and it was there, under the protection of the roof, that they tied their horses.

Pat took Nora's hand and led her around to the front

door of the cottage. He pushed it open, then they went inside.

It was fairly dark inside, as the windows were dirty, but it was surprisingly dry. Nora looked around to take stock of the place that was providing them with shelter. She saw a rough-hewn bed, with a mattress made of cloth-covered straw, a table and two chairs, a chest, and a washstand. There was also a fireplace.

"How did you know this place was here?" Nora asked.

"I've come out here to visit the Forsbergs a few times. That's when I discovered it."

"Oh, a fireplace," Nora said. She shivered. "I wish we could have a fire."

"Ask, and ye shall receive," Pat said. He walked over to the wood box and raised the lid. There were a couple of logs in it, and he took them out and tossed them into the fireplace.

"We'll need something for kindling," he said, and he looked around the room, then settled on a basket made out of woven branches. "This'll have to do." He crushed the basket into small pieces, tossing those in as well. A few moments later, there was a blazing fire going.

"My, I'm impressed," Nora said.

The two stood in front of the fire, enjoying the warmth, which also had the effect of starting to dry their clothes.

"Pat, do you think we're going to have a range war?" Nora asked.

"I don't know. It may well happen."

"Don't you feel guilty about that?"

"Guilty about what?"

"You're selling railroad grant land."

"Nora, that has been the way railroads have financed their construction since the transcontinental railroad was built. The Valley Spur will not survive if I don't have enough money to tide me over until I can establish a revenue stream."

"It's just that I had such high hopes for the railroad," Nora said. "I never thought that it would cause such trouble. To be honest, I'm not sure but what we'd be better off without it."

"You can't stop progress, Nora. Whether I succeed or fail, the railroad will come, and these same problems will have to be faced. Why not solve them now?"

"The rain has stopped," Nora said, without answering Pat's question. "We'd better be going. Papa will be wondering where I am."

CHAPTER THIRTEEN

"Gentlemen," James said quietly and ominously, "I've called you here in secret, because I have something very serious to tell you."

"I know," Cleve said. "Those damned foreign squatters have already cost me half my range land and a quarter of my water. They are squeezing me out of business."

"We're hurting," one of the ranchers said. "But that's really no secret."

"The squatters are a problem, I agree," James said. "But it isn't the squatters I'm concerned about. Not right now, anyway. We have a problem which is much more serious."

"What is that?"

"Come out back with me," James invited. "There is something I want you to see."

The ranchers followed James out of the house and into the barn, curious as to what James was going to show them.

"Professor, I especially want you to see this," he said. "For if the other ranchers concur, I want this incident publicized."

"James, what is it?" Buck asked. "What are you going

to show us?"

"You'll see," James said mysteriously.

Once inside the barn, they walked back to a stall. This stall had been completely walled off and the door was barred shut, separating it from the rest of the barn.

"Sweeney discovered it," James said. "He saw that this animal wasn't even bearing our brand. It was a ringer, run in on us by Pat Flannigan." James pulled the bar, then opened the door. Inside the stall, in the back corner, a single cow stood. The cow was drooling at the mouth, and as it moved around it limped noticeably.

"My God!" Buck exclaimed. He walked into the stall, then kneeled beside the animal and looked at its hooves. "Blisters!" he said. "This animal has hoof and mouth disease!"

The other ranchers drew back in revulsion. "Look at the brand, Buck," James said.

Buck walked around to the animal's rump and looked at the mark which had been burned into its hide.

"It's a slash O," Buck said. "I don't recognize the brand."

"It's not any brand that I know," one of the other ranchers said.

"I don't think it's from the valley."

"In fact, gentlemen, it isn't even from the state," James said. "It's from a herd which was discovered at the feeder-pen lots in Boise, and there it was condemned."

"But I don't understand," Oliver said. "How did this animal get from Boise to our valley?"

"By train," James said simply.

"By train?"

"Think about it," James said. "Flannigan reaches Boise, discovers that we know of his plan to sell off the range land, and in anger, brings all the cows back home. Only he brings us a bonus cow. One cow with hoof and mouth disease. Don't you see? He hoped to infect all five hundred cows on the train, and those cows would in turn infect all the cattle in the valley. We would be wiped out."

"Wiped out? Oh, my God! What are we going to do?" Cleve asked.

The other ranchers expressed the same shock and concern, but James held up his hand to calm them.

"His plan didn't work," James said.

"It didn't work? What do you mean it didn't work? Here is the proof that it did work," Oliver said.

"Take it easy, boys," James said. "There is no chance for other cows to be infected by this one, as long as we keep this one separated."

"Yeah, but what about the beeves it's already been in contact with?"

"They can't be infected until the lesions appear, and we had a lucky break on this. Sweeney saw that the count was off as soon as the cows came back, so he began to check the brands. When he found this strange brand, he pulled it out of the herd. The symptoms didn't start until it was already isolated."

"Well, thank God Flannigan didn't pick an animal that was already infected," Oliver said.

"No," Sterling said quietly. "What he did was worse. Much worse."

"Worse? What do you mean?"

"I was hoping you would realize that, Professor." James said. "Gentlemen," he explained, "it was worse, because Flannigan sent us an animal in disguise. Don't you see? If he had chosen one of the animals that already showed signs of the disease, we would have caught it immediately. Oh, we would have had to destroy the five hundred cows we shipped to Boise, but our herds would have been saved. This way, by choosing an animal he knew had been infected, but was not yet showing the symptoms, there was a chance it would have sneaked through, been exposed to our herds in the valley, and everything would have been lost."

"That sneaky son-of-a-bitch!" Cleve said. "We've got to do something about him, James! Not only does he want to run us out of our range lands, he wants to get rid of us entirely."

"I say we pay the bastard a call," one of the other ranchers said. "Let's burn his damned depot and tear up his track."

"What good would that do?" James asked, as a few of the other ranchers shouted their endorsement of the plan. "He would simply rebuild his depot and relay his track. No, we have to stop him for good."

"Do you have a plan?"

"Yes," James said. He looked at Professor Cassidy. "Professor, are you willing to print what you learned here tonight?"

"Absolutely," Sterling said.

James smiled. "Gentlemen, once this word gets out, Pat Flannigan will never transport another cow for anyone. Public opinion will turn against him so strongly that he will be hard pressed to stay in business. And once Flannigan is out of business, the squatters will be out too. Flannigan is the prime mover. Without him, there will be no new settlers, and the ones who have already come will be forced to leave. What do you think, Professor? Do you agree with me?"

Sterling smiled. "Well, they say the pen is mightier than the sword. I suppose this is where we find out."

"Good," James said. "I can hardly wait until Thursday to read the story."

"You won't have to wait," Sterling said. "I'm going to the office right now. I'll print up an extra edition tonight, and I'll have it on the street by tomorrow morning. The sooner we get rid of Mr. Flannigan, the better off this entire valley will be."

"You won't have any advertising to support this edition, will you?" James asked.

"I don't care. Sometimes service to a community is the foremost requirement of a newspaper."

"I'm glad to hear you feel that way," James said. "It means a lot to me to know you are behind us as a matter of personal conviction." James rubbed his hands together and looked at the others. "Gentlemen, the situation is now in Professor Cassidy's hands, and I can think of no better hands to control our destiny."

"Hear, hear," one of the other ranchers said, and there was modest applause.

"What are you going to do with the infected animal, James?"

"I'm going to destroy it, then bury it in quicklime."

"Don't you think we should keep it as evidence?"

"No, I don't want to take the chance of infecting any other animals," James replied. "You've all seen it; you can act as witnesses if necessary. But after the story, I doubt that will be necessary at all."

"If there is going to be a story, I'd better get back to the office," Sterling said. "I'm going to have to set the plate up myself. I'm certain that Ra is already in bed by now."

The meeting broke up then, and a reflective Sterling rode back into town. He was shocked by his experience tonight. He would not have believed that Pat Flannigan would be capable of such activity if he had not seen the proof with his own eyes. Sterling had written some articles that were hostile to Flannigan and his operation, but only because he believed that the squatters were truly spoiling the good life of the valley. After all, he had left his teaching post and come west, just to enjoy the quality of life offered here, and now Flannigan was going to change all that.

Those articles had been written in good faith, as a genuine expression of displeasure over the changes being wrought, though, and not as a personal attack against Pat Flannigan. Until this evening, Professor Cassidy had believed Pat Flannigan to be, basically, a decent person. In fact, despite their differences, Sterling would have even admitted to liking Pat Flannigan.

But no more. Flannigan's cowardly act of introducing an infected animal to destroy the herds of the entire valley was a crime of unprecedented evil, and he was going to enjoy letting the world know.

Sterling went straight to the newspaper office. He wanted to write the story now, while his blood still boiled with anger. He hoped to capture some of that anger and transfer it to his readers.

Nora was beginning to think that perhaps she and her father were wrong in their relentless attack against the settlers. After all, if she could meet Johan Forsberg and come away with a changed opinion of the man who had been so frightening at the dance, then certainly she could change her opinion about the other settlers. Maybe there could be a peaceful solution after all.

"Oh, Papa, why are you late tonight, of all nights?" she asked aloud.

For the tenth time, she walked to the front window and

peered down the dark street, hoping to see him riding up. That was when she saw a light in the newspaper office. The light had not been there before. That meant that her father, or someone, was there.

Nora turned down the lantern in the living room, then walked down the dark boardwalk to the other end of the street. She saw her father's horse just before she arrived, so the nervousness left her. For some reason he had come back to the newspaper office. Very well, she would just talk to him here.

When Nora stepped inside, her father had just clamped a printer's plate onto the press and was inking the drum.

"What are you doing?" she asked, surprised to see him working so industriously this late at night.

"Ra, wait until you hear," Sterling said. "Never in all my born days have I known anyone as capable of such an abominable act."

"Who?" Nora asked. "Papa, what are you talking about?"

"Read this," Sterling said, printing the first sheet, then handing it to her while the ink was still wet.

Nora read the story quickly, then her look of confusion turned to one of disbelief.

"Dad, you can't really believe Pat had anything to do with this?"

"Is it Pat again?" Sterling asked. He shook his head. "I'm sorry, Ra. But, yes, I have to believe what I have seen with my own eyes. I saw a cow with hoof and mouth disease, and I saw that the brand for that cow was the slash O. That is an Idaho brand. How else would that animal have come to the valley, if not aboard Mr. Flannigan's train?"

Nora shook her head. "He wouldn't do a thing like that," she said. "I know he wouldn't."

"I saw the proof, Nora."

Nora took a deep breath. "All right, I'll stay and help you."

"No," Sterling said. "I'd rather you didn't. In the first place, you seem to be too personally involved right now. The first law of journalism is objectivity. I don't think you can be objective about Flannigan, and there's no sense in subjecting you to any more pain. I want you to go home and get a good night's sleep. Tomorrow things will look better."

CHAPTER FOURTEEN

The residents of Jordan Valley were shocked by the extra release of the newspaper the next day. Sterling had printed twice as many copies as he normally did, and because he wanted maximum exposure, he charged nothing for the paper.

EXTRA   EXTRA   EXTRA
A FOUL DEED

Not in the history of this fair valley has there been a deed of such treachery. It is well known that there has been some difficulty between the ranchers and the immigrant farmers who have settled on the railroad grant land. And while there was a strong wish for cooler heads to prevail, all hope for an equitable settlement has been dashed by the most perfidious deed one could possibly imagine.

That deed so foul, was committed by Patrick Flannigan, the man we had all recently lauded for restoring rail service to the valley. Our readers may recall the joyous event when Mr. Flannigan took cattle to the market. But in a disagreement, he brought the cattle back before they could be marketed, and herein was when the evil action transpired.

Flannigan added one steer to the shipment, AND THAT STEER HAD HOOF AND MOUTH DISEASE! Because the animal bore an Idaho brand, there is no question but that it was intentionally introduced. Fortunately, the poor creature was discovered in time to isolate it from the rest of the herd.

The purpose of this article is to inform all of the malevolence of Mr. Flannigan, and it is the suggestion of this newspaper for all to boycott the railroad until it defaults, and falls into the hands of someone less despicable

Nora took a copy of the newspaper to the depot and found Pat in his office.

"Nora girl, did you talk to the professor about you writing an article telling the side of the immigrants."

"No," Nora replied harshly. "I'm afraid that quite a different article was written."

"You sound so angry, what does that mean?"

"It means that I now know you to be the lowest kind of a person," Nora said. "How could you do such a thing? How *could* you?"

Pat's face mirrored his confusion.

"Nora, I have no idea what you're talking about. What

thing did I do?"

"As if you didn't know about the infected steer," Nora said.

"Infected steer?"

"Are you going to deny that you brought back an infected animal from Idaho, hoping to spread disease through every herd in this valley?"

"Deny it? Of course, I'm going to deny it. Are you trying to tell me that I brought a sick animal here?"

"It's all here, in the extra edition that my father printed today," Nora said. "You put a cow with hoof and mouth disease in the train with the cows James and the others shipped to Boise. You hoped the cow would infect the herds, but it was caught in time and your plan failed."

"You mean the herds aren't infected?"

"No," Nora said. "They are not infected, through no thanks to you."

"Thank God for that," Pat said, breathing a long, audible sigh. "But Nora, you're wrong if you think I had anything to do with this."

"The evidence is overwhelming," Nora said. "Read this."

She thrust the paper in Pat's hand, then turned and left before he could say anything.

* * *

Throughout the rest of the day people read, talked about, and praised Sterling Cassidy for the article.

"I'll tell you what," Sweeney told several others at the Bull Neck Saloon. "That Professor is one brave man, printin' an article like that. Why, there ain't no tellin' what Flannigan is liable to do. I mean, anyone who would bring a sick cow in so as to infect a whole herd? I wouldn't put nothin' by him a' tall."

"Nora, I hardly got any work done today," Sterling told his daughter that evening. "People were coming by all day long to talk to me."

"Well, the good thing I suppose is, that it will certainly make the newspaper popular," Nora pointed out.

"Yes, I suppose so, but..." he paused in mid-sentence

"I know what you were going to say, Papa. You were going to say that you would rather not have gained popularity for the paper in such a way."

"I liked that man. I don't see how we could have been so deceived."

"I know," Nora said, thinking of what she considered her own betrayal.

"Yes, well, you go on home, darlin'. Like I said, I'm going to have to get caught up, tonight."

"All right," Nora said quietly. "Don't work too long. You need your rest."

"I'll be all right; I may even sleep here tonight. I'll be fine, I've napped on the sofa in the office a few times."

"You've napped a *few* times?" Nora teased with a little smile.

"Well, maybe more than a few times," Sterling agreed, returning the smile.

"You know what? After all this, it's good that we can actually find something to smile about," Nora said.

"Good night, darlin'."

"Good night, Papa," Nora replied, kissing her father on his cheek.

What had awakened her? A noise? Yes, in her sleep, she had heard a loud noise, like the sudden peal of thunder. Now she could hear voices, shouting in excitement.

"It's the newspaper office!" one voice said clearly.

"The newspaper office is on fire!" another voice cried.

"Newspaper office?" Nora mumbled sleepily. She got up from the bed and walked over to the window. From the opposite end of the street, she could see a building burning. It *was* the newspaper office!

"Papa!" Nora called. "Papa, come quick, the office is on fire!"

Nora ran to her father's room and knocked on the door. When he didn't answer, she pushed the door open and stepped inside. His bed was empty, and hadn't been slept in.

"Papa?" she said, confused by the fact that he wasn't here. Then she remembered what he had said to her. He told her he might spend the night in the office.

"Papa!" she screamed, this time in fear. She ran through the house, out the front door and down the street toward the burning building. By now there were several dozen people there, and a bucket brigade had been formed.

"My father is in there!" Nora shouted, starting toward the burning building.

"Nora, no!" James said, reaching out to grab her. "You can't go in there! You'd never come out alive!"

"But you don't understand! I *must* go in there!" Nora said, struggling to get out of the grip of the men who held her.

"Do you think your father would want you to lose your own life, trying to save him?"

"I'm sorry, Miss Cassidy, there's nothing we can do," Sheriff Ferrell said. "It's probably too late anyway."

As Nora watched the building burn, she cried bitter tears, thankful that James was there to hold her. The burning building created a glowing circle of light in the black of night. Just beyond the wavering flames, the people of the town were gathered in the darkness, watching in horror as the building collapsed in on itself. Finally, the flames began to die, and gradually the men were able to approach the building.

Nora stood in fearful, almost painful silence, as the men probed through the rubble. Finally, one of them called out something, and the others rushed to him. They stood around in a small group, looking toward the floor. Then one of them walked slowly over to Nora. It was Sheriff Ferrell.

"Miss Cassidy," he started.

"You found him?"

"Yes," the sheriff said. "I'm sorry."

Nora felt dizzy, and she put her hand to her head. Again, James embraced her.

"I'll be here for you, Nora. I'll always be here for you."

"Thank you, James."

"You want some water? The doc is here. Maybe he can give you something to help."

"No, I'll be all right. I would just like to know what happened?" Nora asked. "How did the office catch fire?"

"It was blowed up," one of the men said.

"What?"

"It was blowed up. Someone come ridin' up on a horse, throwed a bomb through the window, and the buildin' was blowed up. Me 'n' Silbey seen it."

"Who would do something like that?" Sheriff Ferrell asked.

"I don' know, Sheriff," the man said. "It was too dark, 'n' we couldn't tell who it was that done it."

"Hey, Sheriff," Sweeny called. "Look at this. We found it in the dirt, right in front of the office."

"What is it?" the sheriff asked.

Sweeny walked over toward the sheriff, holding out a rawhide cord, with an object hanging from it.

"It's a gold nugget on a piece of rawhide," Sweeny said. "Whoever throwed that bomb must've dropped it."

"Hell, Sheriff, they's prob'ly a dozen people in this town could identify that thing for you," Deke said. "That's what the railroad fella, Flannigan, calls his good-luck piece."

"It's not his good-luck piece anymore," the sheriff said. "It's his bad-luck piece. Where's this fella live?"

"He's got a room over at the depot," Sweeny answered. "But you don't expect him to be there, do you?"

"If he's not there, it'll give us a pretty good idea that he did do it, though, won't it?" the sheriff said. "Come on, let's get over there."

The sheriff, followed by an angry mob, hurried over to the depot. They yelled for Pat to come out, but no one answered the call. Finally, the sheriff and a couple of others went inside, but they came out a moment later empty handed.

"He's gone," the sheriff said.

"Well, I reckon that confirms it," another said.

"Let's find that son-of-a-bitch, and when we do, we can get us a rope and string him up!" Sweeny suggested

"No!" Nora screamed.

The crowd looked toward Nora in surprise. "No," she said again. "Please, if you did such a thing you would make a mockery of my father's life. Don't you see? He lived for law and order."

"The girl is right," Sheriff Ferrell said. "We are civilized people here. There will be no lynch mobs as long as I'm the sheriff."

"Well, what do you aim to do, Sheriff?"

"I aim to find Mr. Flannigan," the sheriff said. "And once I find him, I'm going to arrest him. Then we'll get the judge in here, have us a trial, all legal and proper, and if we find him guilty, he will hang."

"What do you mean *if* we find him guilty?" someone shouted, and the others laughed. "You mean *when* we find him guilty, don't you?"

"Maybe so," the sheriff said. "But we have to find him before we can do anything. Now, if any of you men want to ride in a posse, go get your horses and get back here in ten minutes. I'll deputize all of you and we can—"

"Wait a minute, Sheriff," someone suddenly called. "There ain't no need for that."

"What? What are you talking about?"

"Look a'comin'."

They all looked in the direction indicated and saw Patrick Flannigan riding boldly toward them.

CHAPTER FIFTEEN

Pat Flannigan lay on the bunk with his hands folded behind his head, looking at the wall of his jail cell. At some date in the past, an aspiring poet had been confined to these same quarters, and he left his record in the form of a poem.

Friend, here's a verse to help pass your day.
John Price Hampton once came this way.
I took some money that didn't belong to me.
And now it'll be ten long years before they see me free.

"Ah, John Price Hampton, m'boy, where are you now?" Pat asked under his breath.

"Did you say somethin' in there?" the sheriff called out. Sheriff Ferrell was sitting at his desk out front. Pat was the only prisoner.

"I was wondering about John Price Hampton," Pat said. "He left his mark here on your cell wall. Where is he now?"

"He's dead," the sheriff said. "He tried to bust loose when they were takin' him to the pen. Let that be a lesson to you."

"I'll heed the lesson, Sheriff, believe me," Pat said.

The sheriff stood up from his desk, poured himself a

cup of coffee and came over to stand near Pat's cell. "It might make it easier if you tell me what happened," he said, slurping his coffee noisily.

"I told you what happened," Pat said.

"Tell me again."

"After Professor Cassidy put out a special edition, accusing me of introducing hoof and mouth disease into the valley, I was coming to see him, to plead my case and see if I couldn't get him to retract the story."

"I don't doubt that part of it," the sheriff said with a chuckle. "Not a bit. Folks in a cattle raisin' community don't take too kindly to anyone low enough to do somethin' like that."

"That's just it," Pat said. He sat up in bed. "Sheriff, I didn't bring a diseased cow into the valley. At least, not on purpose."

"But you could have, right?"

"I...I don't know," Pat said. "I don't see how one of the condemned cows could have found its way onto the train. I certainly didn't put that cow on the train. That's why I wanted to talk to the professor, to get him to see my side of it."

"Yeah, where were you all day? I know folks were lookin' for you."

"I rode out to see James Wilson. I thought if I could talk to him, I might get an idea on where that cow came from. That's where I had been, when I came riding back to the depot."

"James Wilson says he never saw you," the sheriff said.

"He didn't see me," Pat said. "He wasn't there. None of the ranch hands were there either. The place was completely deserted."

"That's a tough break for you, isn't it?" the sheriff said.

"If one person had been there, you would have an alibi. Now all you have is a motive—and proof that you were there at the newspaper office." The sheriff pulled out the nugget and cord. "On the other hand, we've got motive, opportunity, and this."

"Sheriff, I *admit* that belonged to me. I lost that a couple of weeks ago."

"You mean you lost it a couple of *days* ago, don't you?" the sheriff asked. "When you threw a bomb at the newspaper office?"

"I did not kill Professor Cassidy."

"I'll give you this," the sheriff said. "I don't think you *intended* to kill him. I think you just meant to put him out of business and didn't realize he was sleeping in there. But it doesn't make any difference whether you intended to kill him or not. Burning down the newspaper is a felony, and if anyone is killed during the commission of a felony, whether it is intentional or not, it's murder. You're going to hang for it as soon as you're found guilty."

"You speak as if I've already been tried," Pat said.

"As far as I'm concerned, mister, you have been," the sheriff replied. "All we have to do now is wait for the judge."

"I hope the judge has a better view of justice than you do," Pat said.

The front door of the sheriff's office opened, and Nora stepped into the room. It was the first time Pat had seen Nora since the night he was arrested, though he had asked repeatedly to see her on the day before. He stood up and walked to the bars, then wrapped his hands around them as soon as she came inside.

"Nora!" he said. "Thank God you've come! I've got to talk to you!"

"Miss Cassidy," the sheriff said. "You don't have to come in here if you don't want to. I'm sure seein' this man will only serve to get you more upset. It's goin' to be bad enough at the trial."

"I'm all right," Nora said. She stared pointedly at Pat. "Sheriff, would you excuse us, please? I would like to talk to Mr. Flannigan in private."

"Well, I don't know," the sheriff said. "He's a dangerous man. It might not be such a good idea to let you stay in here alone with him."

"He's behind bars, Sheriff," Nora said. "What can he do? Besides, he's obviously a coward. My father was killed by a bomb thrown in the night. Mr. Flannigan has no bombs with him, does he?"

"No, of course not," the sheriff said. He sighed, then walked over to the rack to take his hat down and put it on. "I'll leave you with him, but you be careful, you hear me?" The sheriff turned to leave; then, just before he exited, he turned back to face Nora. "Listen, Miss Cassidy, you don't have it in mind to ...to do somethin' foolish now, do you?"

"Mr. Flannigan is as safe with me as I am with him," Nora said. "I am willing to wait and allow the law to take its course."

"Good, good," the sheriff said. "I sure wouldn't want to see you get into any kind of trouble, not on top of ever'thin' else that's happened to you."

The sheriff stepped outside and closed the door behind him, and Nora moved over to the cell. As she stared at Pat, there was a hurt, accusing expression on her face which cut through to Pat's very soul.

"I wish you wouldn't stare at me like that," Pat finally said.

"How else should I stare at the man who murdered my

father?" Nora asked.

"Nora, I know it's—"

"Don't call me Nora. My name is Cassidy. Cassidy, do you recognize it? It was the name of a good man."

"He *was* a good man," Pat said. "I can't begin to tell you how sorry I am this happened."

"I don't want your condolences," Nora said bitterly. "You aren't good enough to even mention his name."

Pat sighed. "I did not kill you father," he said. "I hoped you had come here to give me a chance to explain that to you, but evidently that is not the purpose of your visit."

"No, it isn't why I am here."

"Then why have you come?"

"I…I don't know," Nora said. Now her angry eyes filled with tears. "I hoped that, somehow, I could live with my naiveté. To think that I went riding with you, that I was ready to believe you were innocent, on the very day you were to kill my father. I can't help but feel that, somehow, I must share in the blame for his death."

"In that, at least, you are right," Pat said. "You do bear some of the blame for your father's death, and so do I, and so does everyone who has been a party to this whole series of misunderstandings which has brought so much hate."

The door opened again, and this time the sheriff had two people with him. One was a man Pat had never seen, and the other was Mattie Andrews.

"I'm sorry to butt in on you like this, Miss Cassidy, after tellin' you I'd give you some privacy," the sheriff apologized. "But somethin' has come up. Somethin' important, and, if you want my way of thinkin', it's also mighty mysterious." The sheriff looked pointedly at Mattie.

"Mattie, what is it?" Nora asked. "What are you doing here?"

"I've been with the judge," Mattie said, indicating the man with them. "I went to see him as soon as he arrived in town."

"Why?" Nora asked.

"Miss Cassidy, Miss Andrews claims she was with Flannigan on the night your father was killed."

"What?" Nora asked, shocked by the sheriff's words.

"That's right," Mattie said. "Pat Flannigan couldn't have killed Professor Cassidy."

"How do you know?"

"We were together when I heard the bomb explosion," Mattie said quietly.

"Together? What do you mean, together? Where were you?"

"We were...*together*," Mattie said again.

Nora was confused for just a moment, then she gasped and put her hand to her mouth. "Mattie, you mean you were...you and he were..."

"This young lady is willing to testify that she and the prisoner were in bed together at the time of the explosion," the judge said. "And as long as she is willing to testify to that, I can't authorize his further incarceration. I'm ordering you, Sheriff, to set this man free."

"Judge, there's somethin' mighty mysterious about all this," the sheriff said. "How come Flannigan never said anythin' about it before now?"

"Perhaps Mr. Flannigan didn't wish to compromise my reputation," Mattie said. "That is very noble of you, Mr. Flannigan, and I thank you for it. But better that I have a besmirched reputation, than you be wrongly hanged."

"Let him out," the judge said again, and the sheriff opened the cell door, then swung it open.

Pat looked at Mattie, but Mattie wouldn't meet his gaze.

Then he looked at Nora.

"I didn't kill your father," he said quietly.

"I...I *hate* you!" Nora sobbed. She looked at Mattie. "I hate both of you!" she turned and hurried through the door.

The sheriff returned Pat's wallet, but he kept the gold nugget.

"I'm going to have to keep this as evidence until the case is settled," he said.

"That's all right," Pat said. "I don't know that I ever want to see it again, anyway." He started for the door, then he stopped and looked back toward Mattie. She had neither spoken nor looked up since Nora's outburst. "May I walk you to your horse, Mattie?"

Mattie nodded her head and left the office quickly.

"All right," Pat said, as they stood beside Mattie's horse a moment later. "What is this? Why did you ruin your reputation and lie for me?"

"You didn't kill Professor Cassidy, did you?" Mattie asked.

"No, I didn't."

"Then don't look a gift horse in the mouth."

"But I don't understand," Pat said. "Surely there must have been another way you could have come to my aid? Do you think that loudmouthed sheriff is going to keep quiet about all this? He'll drag your name through every gutter and saloon in the county."

"It was the only way I could be sure the judge and the sheriff would believe me," Mattie said. "They wouldn't think I would say such a thing, ruin my reputation, just to provide you with an alibi, if it was false."

"Then why did you?" Pat asked.

Mattie swung onto her horse, then looked down at Pat. Tears were flowing steadily down her face, though she had not sobbed aloud.

"Because I know who did do it," she said. She jerked the reins, turning her horse, then slapped her heels against his flank, urging him into a gallop, before Pat could reply.

The largest crowd ever to gather in one place in Jordan Valley gathered for Sterling Cassidy's funeral that afternoon. There were so many people that they couldn't all be accommodated at St. Martin's Church, so the overflow stood around outside until the service was concluded, then they marched in solemn procession to the graveyard at the edge of town.

Ironically, the graveyard had a clear view of the depot, and Nora, dressed all in black, with a black hat and veil, could see a solitary figure standing on the station platform. She knew that it was Pat, free now, because of the testimony of Mattie Andrews.

Nora had been torn with conflicting emotions ever since Mattie's startling revelation. If Mattie told the truth, that meant that Pat did not kill her father.

Father Crawford pulled at his collar, then stepped up to the open grave as the pine box was lowered into it. When the ropes were pulled away, the priest bent over and picked up a handful of dirt. He dropped it onto the coffin.

"In the sure and certain hope of the resurrection to eternal life through our Lord Jesus Christ, we commend to Almighty God our brother Sterling, and we commit his body to the ground, earth to earth, ashes to ashes, dust to dust. The Lord bless him and keep him, the Lord make his face to shine upon him and be gracious to him, the Lord lift up his countenance upon him and give him peace. Amen."

The mourners began leaving the cemetery and the gravedigger who had been sitting quietly on the other side of the pile of dirt, now came around and began filling in the grave. The dirt made a ringing sound as it left the shovel and a clumping sound as it fell on the box.

Nora had cried for three days, and now there were no tears left. There was just a terrible hollowness inside, and an ache in her heart which she knew could never be erased.

"Nora," James said as he drove her back home in the surrey, "there is something I've been wanting to ask you, and now, I think, would be a good time to do it. With your father dead, you are going to be alone, you are going to need someone you can depend on. You know you can depend on me, don't you?"

"You've always been there for me," Nora said.

James took Nora's two hands into his own. "Then I'm asking you to marry me."

"But what about Mattie?" Nora said. "I've always thought you were going to marry her. I know she's always believed that."

James shook his head. "I've never had any intention of marrying Mattie. I want to marry you."

Nora considered the situation. As James had pointed out, she was alone now, and it would be good to have someone who cared for her, someone she could depend on. She had once harbored fleeting thoughts that that someone might be Pat.

But now, she knew better. Either Mattie lied, and Pat had blown up the newspaper office which killed her father, even if he had no intention of doing so, or Mattie was telling the truth and Pat was in bed with her on the night the newspaper office was bombed. Either way, Nora knew that there was no room in her life for Patrick Flannigan.

"Yes, James," she said, "I will marry you."

CHAPTER SIXTEEN

Pat walked back into the depot, and over to the counter. Ira Chamberlain was standing just on the other side of the counter, marking out sections of land on the large map of the valley.

"Where do you want to put the next group, Pat?" Ira asked.

Pat looked at the map. "Put them down here," he said, pointing to a section of the valley. "They'll have water, and this is good, fertile land. Also, it's far enough from the ranchers that, for the time being at least, we might be able to avoid any further trouble."

"Good idea," Ira said. "In fact, that's probably where I should have put young Forsberg, but he insisted on going in alongside Crooked Creek."

"What?" Pat asked, puzzled by the remark. "What are you talking about?"

"Peter Wemmer and Lars Forsberg came in here yesterday, while you were still in jail. They had the money to buy a piece of land, and they insisted on going alongside Crooked Creek."

"But that'll put them right up against Buckthorn

Ranch," Pat said.

"Yeah, I know. I tried to talk them out of it, but that was where they wanted to go."

"You didn't sell it to them, did you?"

"Well, yes," Ira answered. "Pat, it's already charted. I didn't think it would matter."

"Damn," Pat said. "Those two hotheads up there like that? They're right in the middle of cattle country."

"I'm sorry," Ira said. "I guess I made a mistake."

Pat looked at Ira and smiled. "Well, I guess I could welcome you to the territory," he said. "There's no one around here who's made more dumb mistakes than I have."

"Aren't we going to sell off any of this land?" Ira asked, pointing to the area that ran, like fingers, in between the cattle ranches of the valley.

"I'll sell it," Pat said. "But I didn't want to let that property go until the rest of the tracts were sold. That way, we'd never have anybody stuck out there by themselves. There would at least be safety in numbers."

"Pat, do you think Wemmer and Forsberg are in danger?" Ira asked.

"Not if they're careful," Pat said. He studied the map for a moment and rubbed his chin. "But I'd be willing to bet my last dollar that they aren't being careful at all. In fact, I wouldn't be surprised if they didn't choose that particular piece of land because it *was* a challenge to the ranchers."

"You want me to find something wrong with the deed and run them out of there?" Ira asked.

"No," Pat said. He sighed. "Maybe they're right. Maybe the way to settle this thing is to challenge the cattlemen right off. At least young Wemmer and Forsberg have the courage to do that. I just hope they have common sense to go along with their courage."

"Bring that wire across the draw, Peter, and I'll nail it to this tree. That way we'll have it fenced off," Lars said.

Lars Forsberg and Peter Wemmer were working with a roll of barbed wire, fencing off the perimeters of their land. They were wearing denim trousers and jackets and heavy leather gloves, to protect them from the barbs that protruded from the heavy roll of wire in the back of the wagon.

Peter giggled as he brought a length of wire across the small gulley and handed it to Lars.

"How many cows you think we have trapped in here?" he asked.

"About twenty or so, I'd say," Lars replied. He cut the wire with a large pair of wire cutters, then wrapped a strand around the trunk of a tree and began hammering it into place. "Just enough to pay back some of the damage they've done."

"It ain't like we're stealin' neither," Peter said. "After all, these cows come onto our own territory all by themselves. We didn't do nothin' to bring them here."

"But we're sure doin' somethin' to keep 'em here," Lars said, laughing. He finished putting the wire up, then stood back and looked at it, reaching out to test the tension of the strands.

"We've got to do something," Peter said. "It's for sure no one else will. All the homesteaders are like a bunch of old women. They moan and groan ever' time some cowman runs over 'em, but they don't do nothin' about it."

"I've got an idea," Lars said.

"What is it?" Peter asked. "If it's as good an idea as this, I'm all for it."

"Back before any of the rest of the folks come into the

valley, when they was just us Forsbergs and you Wemmers, and a couple more families, the cowmen put up signs, warning us off the graze land, remember? They told us they would destroy our crops, tear down our fences, and burn our buildin's and such."

"Yeah, I remember."

"Let's put up signs here, tellin' the cattlemen that we will kill any cow that wanders onto our land. We got a right to do that."

"Yeah," Peter said. "Let's serve notice on them. We'll let them know that here's two homesteaders that won't be run off or buffaloed."

There was a low rumble of thunder in the hills, and both men looked toward them, to see a rapidly building thunderhead.

"We'd better get out of this draw before the rains come," Lars suggested.

"I'll get the tools," Peter replied.

Both men began to work quickly, picking up the tools and extra wire and throwing them in the back of the wagon. Then, just as they were ready to leave, there was the cracking sound of a bullet smashing through the side of the wagon, and the loud roar of a rifle shot.

"Hold it, boys!" a voice called from behind them.

Peter and Lars froze in their tracks.

"Well, well, well, now look here, would you?" a taunting voice said. There was a sound of horse hooves on the rocks, and Peter and Lars turned to see half a dozen riders approaching them slowly. All were armed with rifles, held out in plain sight, ready for use, should the need arise.

"You men are trespassin'," Peter said angrily.

The leader of the riders smiled and looked at the others. The leather of his saddle squeaked as he twisted around toward them.

"Did you men hear that?" he asked. "These here fellas think we're trespassin'."

The armed riders laughed.

"Mister, this here is range land," the leader of the group said. "It always has been, and it always will be." He pointed his rifle toward the strands of wire which had been stretched across the draw. "Now you tell me what the hell that is for."

"It's to protect our property," Lars said.

"To keep your damn cows out," Peter added.

One of the riders swung down from his horse and examined a cow pile. He looked up toward the leader of the group.

"Sweeney, I'll tell you the truth, it looks to me like these fellas is tryin' to keep a few cows in. Look at this."

The one called Sweeney got off his horse and walked over to examine the cow pile. He looked toward Peter and Lars.

"Is that right?" he finally asked. "Have you fellas stretched a little wire to keep some cows in?"

"Yes," Peter said defiantly. "There are a few head of cattle trapped in here, and we aim going to keep 'em 'til we're paid for the damages you've done to our property."

Sweeney looked around, at the draw, the trees, and the rapidly climbing terrain to the hills which formed the walls of the draw.

"Now, except for the devil's wire that you two galoots stretched across here, this here land is just the way God made it. What makes you think we done any damage?"

"We're talking about our families," Lars said. "And the other homesteaders of the valley. They've had their crops ruined, their barns burned, and their fences torn down."

"I see," Sweeney said. "Well, fellas, it's like this. When we do those things, I don't figure we're doin' any damage at all. I figure we're just puttin' things back the way God made 'em in the first place."

"Who made you God's avengin' angels?" Lars asked bitterly.

Sweeney smiled, and looked toward the others. "Hey, that's a good name, isn't it? Whyn't we call ourselves the Avengin' Angels?"

Everyone laughed, except Peter and Lars. Then, after the laughter had died, the smile left Sweeney's face, and he pointed to the wagon. "Slim, you'n Deke, take that wagon up to the overhang up there, and push it over. That ought to bust it up enough that they can't use it to haul any more barbed wire."

"What about the horses?" Slim asked.

"Spook 'em, 'n' run 'em off," Sweeney said. "Maybe a walk back home would do these galoots some good."

It started to rain then, just a few drops at first, then a steady, heavy downpour. The armed riders began to pull their slickers out of the saddlebags.

"You two," Sweeney said. "Pull down that wire."

Two riders rode over to the fence and threw ropes around the center pole. They pulled until the pole snapped, and the wire popped out of the trees on each side of the draw. There was a cheer from the others when the fence came down.

Peter and Lars stood helplessly in the rain, watching as the fence was pulled up and then, a moment later, as their wagon went crashing down over the edge of a nearby cliff. The wagon smashed and splintered into pieces as it hit.

"Now," Sweeney said, pointing his rifle at the two men, "git outta them clothes."

"What?" Peter asked.

"I said shuck outta them clothes," Sweeney said. "I think a walk home in the rain is just what you need to cool you off."

Peter and Lars hesitated for a moment, so Sweeney fired a shot, hitting the ground between them. The bullet kicked mud up on them, then careened off through the valley, whining as it did so.

"Get 'em off," Sweeney said menacingly.

Peter and Lars glared angrily at the riders, but they took their clothes off. Sweeney picked them up.

"Now, we're goin' to ride on back and find our cows," he explained. "We'll leave these clothes wherever we find the cattle. You fellas are lucky. Normally, we hang cattle rustlers, right on the spot. And if we ever catch you with any more of our cows, we'll hang you."

Sweeney shouted to the others, and the cowboys rode off, sending back one last, defiant shout.

Peter and Lars, naked and exposed to the rain and the elements, started walking back.

"I'm goin' to kill that son of a bitch," Lars swore.

"Who?" Peter asked. "The one they call Sweeney?"

"No," Lars answered. "I'm goin' to kill James Wilson. He's the one behind all this."

CHAPTER SEVENTEEN

The fire that killed Professor Cassidy and burned the newspaper office also destroyed the printing press, type, paper, ink, woodcuts, and all the other equipment and materials stored in the building. Because of that, Jordan Valley was without a newspaper for three weeks after the fire, and Nora Cassidy was without anything to keep her mind off what happened.

One day, shortly after her father's funeral, a man knocked on Nora's door. He arrived in the middle of a late summer rainstorm brought on by a chinook wind. Nora wondered who would come to see her in the midst of such foul weather.

"My name is Eblem, Miss Cassidy," the man said, when Nora opened the door. "I've brung you a printing press, plates, type, paper, ink, ever'thin' you need to get back in operation."

"What?" Nora gasped.

"Yes, ma'am, it's all out there on the wagon," the man said.

Nora looked around the man and saw a wagon standing in the street in front of her house. The back of the wagon consisted of lumps covered with a canvas cover. Ropes held the cover secure.

"Who are you?" Nora asked. "Where did you come from?"

"I told you, miss," the man said. "My name is Eblem. Newt Eblem. I'm a freight operator from Bakertown, 'n' I come all the way here carryin' this here load. It took me two days, so I hope there ain't no trouble with it."

"But...I don't understand," Nora said. She was confused. Why was this equipment being delivered? "You see, I didn't order any such equipment. Indeed, I can't even pay for it."

"You don't have to pay nothin' for it, ma'am, it's already paid for," Eblem replied. "Even the freight's been paid. All you got to tell me is where I can put it?"

"Wait a minute," Nora said, suspiciously. "Who paid for it?"

"I don't know, ma'am," Eblem said. "But maybe this will tell you. I'm supposed to give you this here letter."

Eblem pulled an envelope from his inside pocket and handed it to Nora. It was damp, though it had remained dry enough to be legible.

"Please," Nora said, "come in."

"No, thankee, ma'am," Eblem said. "I been out in it so long now that I don't even notice the rain. Besides, I'd just be gettin' your house all muddied up an' ever'thin'. What I'd really like to do is get this stuff delivered somewhere so's I could go into the saloon and get me somethin' to ward off the cold an' the wet, iffen you get my drift."

"Oh, uh, take it...take it to Miller's Emporium," Nora said. "He has a place in the back of his store which he offered to let me use, right after the fire. Of course, I didn't have anything to put there then, so I couldn't take him up on his kind offer."

"Yes'm," Eblem said, tipping his hat. "Miller's Emporium. I'll get all this stuff unloaded there."

> *Dear Miss Cassidy:*
>
> *Words cannot express the sorrow we of the Baker Daily Register felt, when we learned of the tragic death of our friend and colleague, Sterling Cassidy.*
>
> *Your father's death has left a void which cannot soon be filled. His voice has been stilled, his wisdom taken from us, and we all share in your loss.*
>
> *It is enough that our state has lost the company of this great man, but we should not have to suffer the loss of the fine newspaper he founded. Therefore, I beg of you to accept from an admirer of your father's, this gift of equipment which will allow you to publish the Valley Monitor again. You can understand that your benefactor wishes to remain anonymous, but this generous person and the admirers of the Valley Monitor hope you will accept.*
>
> *Sincerely,*
> *Tom Post,*
> *Publisher*

Tears came to her eyes as she read the letter. So, thanks to some unknown but very kind soul, her father's paper could continue! The *Valley Monitor* would be published again!

Nora threw on a coat, then ran joyfully, through the

muddy street and the pouring rain to Miller's Emporium. It was the first moment of joy she had allowed herself since her father's death.

Nora walked over to the press and rested her hand lightly on the platten. She looked at the type cases and the rows of clean, never-before used letters. Tears of happiness came to her eyes.

Miller put his hand on Nora's shoulder.

"I'm glad," he said. "I'm glad for you, and for the town, that we will have a newspaper again."

Nora took off her raincoat and hung it from a hook. "We won't have one unless I get to work," she said. "There's a lot to do to get the first paper out."

* * *

"Boss, I found another slaughtered steer," Sweeney told James, at about the same time Nora was beginning to work on the paper.

"Where?"

"Down at the South Fork," Sweeney said. "And it's on our land too. I mean, this critter wasn't anywhere near the range land. Whoever kilt him come right onto our place 'n' done it. And here's the strange part, boss. *They didn't even take no meat.*"

"What?" James asked, rising from his chair. He had been working on the ranch ledger when Sweeney came to him with the news, but not until Sweeney told him the last part of it did he really become upset. "They didn't take any meat?"

"Not so much as one steak," Sweeney said.

"Damn!" James said, hitting his desk with his fist.

"Why you reckon someone'd go to all the trouble of sneakin' onto the ranch 'n' killin' a steer, then not even take any meat from it?" Sweeney asked. "It's pure bewil-derin', if you ask me."

"It isn't bewildering at all," James said. "Whoever killed that cow did it from malice, not from need. It was some low-life squatter's way of getting at us."

"He couldn't of been very smart," Sweeney said. "Hell, boss, he left tracks a blind man could follow."

James reached for his hat. "Take me to it, Sweeney. Let's see if we can find him."

The rain continued to fall as the two horsemen rode through the rugged gullies and draws that led down to the South Forks. Both men wore ponchos and had the brims of their hats turned down to keep the rain away, but they were soon soaked to the skin.

Finally, James saw the animal, a mound of brown and red, as they approached. Two cougars were tearing at the meat, so intent on their unexpected feast that they didn't even notice the arrival of the men. James held out his hand, then slipped his rifle from his saddle holster.

"I'll take the one on the right," he said. "You take the one on the left. We'd better fire at the same time, or we'll spook 'em."

"I'll count three," Sweeney said, pulling his own rifle from the holster.

Sweeney counted quietly, then two rifles roared as one. Both cats twisted around, then fell, twitching. When the two men rode up to the cow, Sweeney finished off both cats with his pistol.

"Sweeney, are you sure the cats didn't get to this ani-mal?" James asked. "It's pretty well torn up."

Sweeney pointed to the head of the steer.

"Not unless cougars have suddenly learned how to use guns," Sweeney said. "This cow was shot through the head with a Winchester thirty-thirty."

"Yeah," James said. "I see what you mean."

"And there are the tracks," Sweeney pointed out, indicating hoof prints which stretched out across a muddy field as deep as if the field were plowed.

"All right," James said. "Let's follow them." Sweeney and James started along the trail, riding at a fairly rapid gait. Finally, they approached a box canyon.

"He went in here," Sweeney said. "Come on, let's go take him out of there."

"Wait a minute," James cautioned. He pulled his horse up short.

"What's wrong?" Sweeney said. "Come on, boss, he's in there. Don't you see the tracks?"

"Why is he in there?" James asked.

"Why? I don't know. Why did he kill the cow and not take the meat? 'Cause he's a dumb sodbuster, that's why."

"Maybe he's not as dumb as we think," James said.

"Why? What do you mean?"

"I think this fella, whoever he is, is trying to lead us into a trap. Look, that's a natural ambush."

"Yeah," Sweeney said. "You're right."

"I'll tell you what. You circle on around that way, so you can come up behind those rocks. I'll go right on in. If there's anyone waiting, we'll soon know about it."

"All right," Sweeney said. He looked toward the rocks that formed the natural fortress. "I'll get up there and wave. You don't start in until you see me."

James waited until Sweeney was in position, and when he saw the cowboy wave, he started on into the narrow gorge, following the tracks.

"That's far enough, Wilson!" a voice suddenly called.

James stopped. From behind the rocks, a man stood up.

James recognized him as Lars Forsberg.

"So," James said, "you're the one who killed my steer."

"That's right, Wilson," Lars said. "I thought it would bring you around."

"Well you thought right," James said. He saw Sweeney coming up slowly behind Lars. "Does your dad know about this?"

"Leave my dad out of it," Lars said. "I'm my own man."

"Yeah, I can see," James said. "Killing a dumb animal for no reason is a very manly thing to do."

"I didn't kill it for no reason," Lars said. "I had a reason. I had a good reason."

"Would you mind telling me what that reason is?" James asked. Behind Lars, Sweeney drew closer.

"I wanted to get you in here," Lars said.

"All right, you got me here. Now, what do you intend to do with me?"

Lars smiled, an evil smile, and he raised a pistol. "I aim to kill you, mister," he said.

James looked toward Sweeney. Sweeney was still too far away to be of any help, though he was moving steadily down the rocks toward Lars. James felt his hair stand on end, and a nervous roll in the pit of his stomach.

"Why?" he asked. "Why do you want to kill me?" *Keep him talking,* James thought. *Anything to buy a little more time.*

Lars laughed a wild, demented laugh. "You ask me that? You have destroyed crops, burned barns, pulled down fences, beaten farmers, and you ask why I want to kill you?"

"Listen, son," James said.

Lars cocked the pistol and pointed it at James. "Don't call me son!" he said. "Only my father can call me son!"

"I'm sorry," James said. "It's just that you're so young, and I see you making such a mistake."

"I'm not too young."

"How old are you? Eighteen, nineteen?"

"Twenty," Lars answered.

"Lars, you aren't going to live to see twenty-one if you go through with this. You'll be caught, and you'll be hanged."

"I don't care," Lars said. He took careful aim. "You'll be in hell before me."

James felt a sudden panic. He was about to be shot! He made a dive for a nearby rock just as Lars's gun went off. He felt the bullet tear into his shoulder, and a searing pain like that of a branding iron pierced his flesh. He hit the ground, then rolled behind a rock.

"Forsberg!" Sweeney called, and Lars, surprised by the shout from behind, turned around and fired wildly toward Sweeney. Sweeney was armed with a rifle, and thus had the advantage over Lars. Sweeney raised the rifle, took careful aim, and squeezed the trigger.

James heard the boom of the rifle, and then the echo returning from the canyon walls. Lars pitched back, head down, and slid down the hill. His pistol bounced and clattered over the rocks, reaching the bottom before he did.

James grabbed Lars's pistol, then stood up and pointed it toward the young man, who came sliding and bouncing behind it. Finally, Lars's body stopped its slide and James walked over to it, still holding the pistol pointed toward it.

"No need for that," Sweeney called from halfway up the side. He was working his way down methodically. "He's dead. I hit 'em plumb center."

James dropped to one knee and looked into Lars's face. His eyes were open, but opaque. His mouth was twisted grotesquely. There was a hole in his chest, and the rain-diluted blood washed away in bright red.

"You're right on that," James said. He dropped the pistol and clutched his shoulder.

"Are you all right, boss?" Sweeney asked.

"Yeah," James said, "but it hurts like the blazes."

"Let me take a look at it," Sweeney offered. He cut the hole in James's shirt wider and stared at it.

"How is it?" James asked.

"It's pretty deep. I'd better get you in town to a doctor."

"No!" James said.

"No? Boss, what are you talkin' about? That bullet's got to come out."

"Take me home," James said. "You can get a doctor to come out to Buckthorn. He can treat me there."

"All right," Sweeney said. "You're the boss. What about this hombre? Are you going to just leave him here?"

James looked down at Lars. The rain fell into his open eyes, but Lars was beyond flinching.

"Tell the sheriff about him," James said. "Tell the sheriff to come see me, I'll give him the full story. Now, help me onto my horse."

The pain stopped shortly after James was on his horse, and numbness set in. The numbness was a blessing, because it allowed James to stay on his horse for the ride back. But it also brought on weakness, so that by the time they reached the house, James was only barely cognizant of what was going on around him.

Sweeney put James in bed, then left to get the doctor. James passed out shortly after that and didn't come to until he felt hands pulling and pushing and poking him.

"Oh," he moaned.

"Well," Dr. Groves said. "It's good to see that you're

still alive."

"What are you doing?" James asked groggily.

"I'm cleaning your wound," Dr. Groves said. "I've already removed the bullet."

"You...you've already taken it out?"

"Yep," the doctor said. He picked up a red-soaked piece of gauze, and James saw the bullet, misshapen from its impact with his body. "A forty-four caliber, from the looks of it." He dropped the bullet with a clink into the pan of water. The water swirled red.

"By tomorrow the worst of it will be over," Dr. Groves said. "Like as not, there was some infection set in. You'll be running a fever tonight. Tonight is when you need a nurse."

"A nurse?"

Doctor Groves sighed. "I thought you might be a mite obstinate. So I brought someone else to do the nursing chores. That is, if you don't mind."

James felt himself growing dizzy again. "Yeah," he heard himself say. It sounded as if his voice were coming to him from a great distance...there was a hollowness to it.

"Good," Dr. Groves said. He turned toward the door. "You can come on in now."

The door opened, and James, as if staring through a thick fog, looked to see who was coming in.

It was Mattie Andrews.

CHAPTER EIGHTEEN

Mattie sat in a chair beside James's bed while he slept. She kept a basin of water handy, and when he was feverish, she bathed his forehead with cool water to bring it down. When he got chilled, she put more quilts on him. When he tossed restlessly, she took his hand and held it tenderly.

"Oh, James," she said quietly. "If only you knew why I told that lie about being with Flannigan on the night Cassidy was killed."

Mattie thought back to that fateful night, reconstructing the events in her mind.

"Are you absolutely certain it is hoof and mouth disease?" she had asked her father when he returned from the meeting James had conducted.

"Of course, I'm sure," Buck replied. "The animal had blisters on its hooves, and it was foaming at the mouth. What other evidence do you need?"

"More evidence than that," Mattie replied. "There are diseases which look like hoof and mouth, but really aren't. I learned that from Dr. Newberry."

"Well, Dr. Newberry has been dead for two years now,

and we only have our own wits to go on," Buck said. "My wits tell me it is hoof and mouth."

"I'm going to see for myself," Mattie said. Mattie rode over to the Buckthorn Ranch. It was a pleasant ride. The rain had washed everything clean, and the stars twinkled brightly.

When Mattie reached Buckthorn, she was surprised to see that the house was totally dark. She knocked on the door but got no answer. Even the bunkhouse was empty.

As Mattie thought about it, however, it seemed less strange, for surely James and the others were checking the herds closely, to make certain there were no other signs of the disease.

Mattie went out to the barn. She opened the stall, lit a lantern, and examined the sick animal closely. Its eyes were clear, and its nose clean. In fact, there seemed to be no soreness, nor foaming of the mouth, though her father had told her that there had been foaming when he had seen it. The hooves were covered with blisters, though, and Mattie bent down to examine them more closely.

There was something strange about this. The blisters had an unusual pattern to them. She wished Dr. Newberry were still alive or had lived long enough to allow her to complete the course in veterinary medicine she was taking from him.

"I wish you could talk," she said softly to the cow. She patted it on the head, and it nudged against her, as if grateful for some tender consideration.

Mattie sighed, and started to leave, when she saw something in the corner of the stall, covered by burlap bags. She walked over to look at it more closely and saw that it was just a branding iron.

She laughed. *James will be wondering where this is,*

come branding time. She picked it up, and as she did so, she heard a bottle clink. She laid the iron down and flipped the burlap bag aside. Beneath the bag she saw a bottle of sulphuric acid.

"What in the world?" she asked aloud.

Mattie picked up the bottle and examined it. Now what would James want with sulphuric...suddenly Mattie looked over toward the cow. Sulphuric acid! Sulphuric acid on the hooves would give the symptoms of hoof and mouth disease!

Mattie picked up the branding iron and noticed then that the brand wasn't the Buckthorn brand at all. It was a slash Zero, the same brand that was on the supposedly sick cow. James had faked the entire thing. *But why?*

Mattie went back to the house, then into the kitchen. She found some baking soda, took it back to the barn and made up a baking soda and water solution. She bathed the poor animal's hooves in the solution, hoping to give it some relief from the cruel pain it must be suffering from the acid.

Mattie had just finished when she heard horses arriving outside. She extinguished the lantern, poured out the baking soda solution, and left the stall, just as James and Sweeney came into the barn. She stood in the shadows, unnoticed by either of them.

Sweeney laughed. "Did all the boys look for other signs of the disease?"

"Yes," James said. "They and the other ranchers are all scared to death. They figure every other cow is infected."

"It worked fine, boss. You have everyone in the valley thinkin' Flannigan brought that cow in here. He's gonna be 'bout the most unpopular man that ever set foot in Oregon."

"What about tonight, did it go all right?"

"It went fine," Sweeney said. "This on top of the hoof 'n mouth will be about enough to get him run out on a rail. But I'll tell you one thing, the professor sure ain't gonna take to havin' his place burned down like that. I felt kinda bad doin' it."

"I'll build him a newer and bigger newspaper plant," James said. "Then he can print how Flannigan was so upset by his exposure of binging in this diseased cow that he bombed the newspaper office. Don't worry about the professor, I'll take care of him. What about the gold nugget? Did you leave it where it could be found?"

"Right out front, boss, just like you said. When they find it, Flannigan will get the blame."

"All right, only one more thing to do," James said. "You'd better take the steer out and shoot it, then bury it in quicklime."

"Seems a shame to shoot a healthy steer," Sweeney said.

"Look at it this way," James said. "The poor critter has to be suffering from that acid. You'll be doing it a favor."

"Yeah," Sweeney said. "I guess you're right."

Mattie waited until she could leave without being seen. Then she rode back home, sick at heart, and confused in her mind. When she learned that Professor Cassidy had been in the building when it burned, she knew that James's plan had backfired. It was going to go much further than he intended, because it would result in Pat Flannigan being hanged for murder.

Mattie couldn't let Pat Flannigan be hanged for a crime he didn't commit, but she couldn't save him at the expense of James's freedom. She knew that James and Sweeney were unaware that the professor would be in the newspaper office. In fact, she had overheard James tell Sweeney he would build a new office. That made the professor's death an accident. An accident for which Mattie thought neither man should have to suffer. Thus, she decided to provide Pat with an iron-clad, though costly, alibi.

"What time is it?" James asked as he thrashed restlessly on the bed.

The question startled Mattie, not only because it came in the middle of the night, after hours of silence, but also because his voice was clear and strong.

"I heard the hall clock strike three a short time ago," Mattie said.

"Why are you here?" James asked.

"You needed a nurse," Mattie answered simply.

"But why would you want to nurse me?" James asked. "I thought you were in Pat Flannigan's camp."

"Oh, James, I..."

When the sheriff halted the wagon, he looked toward the Forsbergs' house. In the back of the wagon, wrapped in canvas, lay the body of their son. This was not a moment he relished.

The wagon tilted under his weight when he stepped down, and as he started toward the house, the front door opened, and Johan Forsberg walked out onto the porch.

"Mornin', Sheriff," Johan said. He was rolling his shirtsleeves up, exposing massive forearms. "What can I do for you?"

"Mr. Forsberg," the sheriff said. He paused, then took out his handkerchief and wiped his forehead. "I'm afraid I have some sad news to report."

"Sad news?" Forsberg said. "What sort of sad news?"

"It's about your son," the sheriff said. He cleared his throat, then pointed to the wagon. "I have him here."

Johan looked toward the wagon and noticed, for the first time, the form under the canvas.

"Mrs. Forsberg," Johan called.

Mrs. Forsberg stepped to the front door of the house. She had a pleasant smile on her face, but as soon as she saw her husband's expression, she knew something was wrong.

"What is it, Mr. Forsberg?" she asked.

"It's Lars," Johan said, pointing to his covered form in the sheriff's wagon.

"*Lars!*" Mrs. Forsberg screamed, and she ran to the wagon and began pulling at the canvas, crying, and calling his name, over and over.

"What happened?" Johan asked.

"There was an accident," said the sheriff.

"An accident? What? Did he fall or something?"

"Oh, Johan, our Lars was shot!" Mrs. Forsberg suddenly screamed, so distraught that for the first time in over twenty-five years of marriage she used her husband's Christian name. She had pulled the canvas back and could see the bullet hole in his chest.

"What's that? Shot, you say?" Johan said. He moved quickly to the wagon, then looked down at the body of his son. He turned back toward the sheriff with anger on his face. "I thought you said it was an accident," he challenged.

"It was, Mr. Forsberg," the sheriff replied.

"What kind of accident is it that would get a fella shot?" Johan demanded.

"The kind of accident when a man goes where he has no business goin'," the sheriff replied.

"What? Are you telling me someone shot my son because he was trespassing?"

"No," the sheriff said. "I'm not sayin' that at all. It really was an accident. You see, one of the ranchers was havin' some trouble with cougars. The cats were attackin' their cattle. So, a couple of men went out to hunt the cougars. They tracked them into a narrow gorge, then they shot both of them. They killed the cougars all right; fact is, I've got their hides down to the office as evidence. But your son was holed up in that draw, nobody knows why, and he caught a stray bullet."

"Where was the draw?" Johan asked.

"That's what I mean when I say he was where he had no business bein'. That draw was right there on the ranch."

"Which ranch?"

"Which ranch? Well, it don't really make any difference, does it? The point is, your boy is dead, and ever'body concerned is plumb sorry about it."

"Which ranch?" Johan demanded.

"All right, I'll tell you which ranch," the sheriff finally said. "But I'm warnin' you Mr. Forsberg. You let this here matter be, do you hear me? I've already investigated it, and I'm convinced it happened just like I told you it did."

"Which ranch?"

"The Buckthorn."

"That's James Wilson's place, ain't it?"

"Yes."

"I might have known." Johan scooped Lars's body up from the back of the wagon and started toward the house with it, carrying it as easily as he had when Lars was a child.

"Mr. Forsberg, I gotta ask you," the Sheriff Ferrell said. "What are you plannin' on doin'?"

"I'm plannin' on buryin' my boy," Johan replied without looking around.

"After that," the sheriff called out to him. The sheriff was standing alone now, for Mrs. Forsberg had walked alongside her husband, holding Lars's hand, and crying. "After that, what are you plannin' on doin'?"

"My thanks, Sheriff, for bringin' the boy to me," Johan called back. Johan and his wife went inside the house and closed the door behind them.

The sheriff stood there for a moment. Then, with a sigh, he climbed onto the seat of the wagon, snapped the reins, and started back toward town.

The first issue of the *Valley Monitor* after the fire carried a blank white column, bordered in a heavy black line. At the top of the column beneath the title, *Polecat,* there was printed: *Sterling Stowe Cassidy,* 1832-1881.

It was a fitting tribute to her father, one which was much more appropriate than anything Nora could have written.

Nora also carried the story of the accidental shooting death of young Lars Forsberg. She remembered the meal she had eaten with the Forsberg family, and she recalled the intensity of the young man. She felt a deep sympathy for the Forsbergs, and she wrote the story with tender concern for their feelings, concluding with a genuine expression of sympathy.

Pat attended the funeral, along with more than two hundred other settlers. There was a general feeling that "one-of their own" had been killed, and there was a large turn-out to lend support to the Forsberg family.

"I'll tell you one thing," Peter Wemmer told Pat, "Lars's gettin' kilt was no accident."

"How do you know?" Pat asked.

"I just know," Peter said. "He told me he was goin' out to Buckthorn to see James Wilson personally. If you want my thinkin' on it, James Wilson kilt him, and he did it of a pure purpose."

"Peter, I know there are hard feelings between the ranchers and the farmers. But I don't think it has come *this* far," Pat said.

"Yes, it has," Peter said. "I know it for a fact."

"That kind of talk does no one any good," Pat cautioned. "You don't know it for a fact unless you actually watched it happen. Did you see it happen?"

"No," Peter said. "But I know Wilson kilt Lars."

"How can you be so sure of such a thing?" Pat asked in desperation.

"'Cause Lars went up there to kill Wilson," Peter said.

"What? Why would he do such a thing? I mean, I know that Lars was often a hothead about things, but I thought he would have more sense than to try something like that."

"You don't know what me 'n' Lars had to put up with that very day."

"Tell me about it."

"Me 'n' Lars was workin' some fence when a bunch of no count cowboys jumped us. They were ornery cusses, every'one, 'n' they jumped us and tore down the fence. Then they made us take off all our clothes 'n' walk back naked."

"Was Wilson with them?"

"No," Peter said, "he weren't with 'em. Fact is, we don't even know that it was Wilson's men. But Lars said that Wilson was to blame just the same, 'cause all the cattle ranchers listened to what he had to say."

"Lars was correct on that score," Pat said. "Wilson does call all the shots. But to go up there with the express purpose of killing James Wilson was a dumb thing to do."

"Yeah," the sheriff told Pat when Pat went to see him after the funeral. "I know Lars Forsberg tried to kill Wilson.

He slaughtered one of James's cows, and when James and Sweeney went to investigate, Forsberg jumped 'em, and took a shot at them. In fact, James got hit. He's at home now, recuperating from a bullet wound in the shoulder. Sweeney got Lars before Lars could do any more damage."

"Then why did you tell Mr. Forsberg that Lars was shot by accident?" Pat asked.

"Mr. Flannigan, do you want to see a range war out here?"

"No, of course not."

"Well, sir, that's just what you'd have if Forsberg knew that Lars was shot by Sweeney, self-defense or no. I figured this was the easiest way to keep the lid on things, and if you got any concern about peace in this valley, you'll go along with it."

"I see your point, Sheriff," Pat said. "But I don't agree with what you're doing."

CHAPTER NINETEEN

"Nora," Pat greeted, when she showed up at the depot. "Or should I address you as Miss Cassidy?"

"Miss Cassidy will do for now," Nora replied. "Though it shall soon become Mrs. Wilson."

"You...you're going to marry Wilson?"

"I am, sir."

Pat was upset by Nora's news, though he knew he had no right to be. He was sure that she blamed him for her father's death, whether he actually threw the bomb or not. And why shouldn't she blame him? There had been no trouble in the valley until he brought it.

"And so you came to share that news with me?"

"No, I'm writing an article, and I came to get your opinion on the cattlemen's plan to drive their herd to Boise, rather than use your railroad."

"I have no opinion, Miss Cassidy," Pat said, without further amplification of his comment.

Article in the Valley Monitor:
        CATTLEMEN TO DRIVE
        HERDS TO BOISE

The Valley Cattlemen's Association announced this week, that they would unite their herds for one, massive drive to the rail head at Boise. Any unemployed cowboy who wishes to take temporary work in helping with the drive may apply to James Wilson of the Buckthorn Ranch. Mr. Wilson reports that this will be the biggest cattle drive in the history of the valley, and many extra hands will be required for a successful drive.

When asked why the cattlemen were driving their herds to Boise, rather than taking advantage of existing railroad service, the cattlemen replied that the railroad had adopted policies which were detrimental to the cattlemen's interest, and could not be used as a vehicle for shipping cattle. Mr. Flannigan, of the Valley Spur Railroad, made no comment.

"So, I made no comment, huh?" Pat said under his breath. "It's a little hard to make a comment when I'm not asked the question." Pat was in the Bull's Neck Saloon, standing at the back end of the bar, having a drink. He had come in to think about the article which had appeared in this week's newspaper. He wasn't concerned about the loss of business from the cattlemen, because the farmers would soon be shipping their harvests to market and that would allow the railroad to survive.

Pat was concerned, though, about the continual worsening of the relationship between the railroad and the older, established inhabitants of the valley. For a railroad to survive in the long term, it had to have a good relationship with everyone, and the animosity which had developed between the settlers and the ranchers, and the ranchers and the railroad, was bad. That relationship would continue to deteriorate, as long as such articles continued to appear in the newspaper. And that responsibility, Pat laid squarely on Nora Cassidy.

It was late, and much of the early evening crowd in the Bull's Neck had already left. The only remaining customers were the serious drinkers, the drifters who had no other place to go, and the men who were waiting for their turn to visit one of the "soiled doves" of the establishment. Two of the latter were cowboys, standing at the opposite end of the bar from Pat. Pat knew them as Deke and Slim, and he knew also that they were with the ones who jumped Lars and Peter.

"Hey, bartender," Deke called out. "Bartender did you happen to check Flannigan's shoes?"

"Check his shoes?" the bartender replied.

"Yeah," Deke said. He held his nose. "Smells to me like he's been walking around in pigpens. Why don't you look at his shoes?"

"Is that right, Flannigan?" Slim asked, laughing. "Have you been suckin' up to your pig-farmin' friends? You been playin' in their pigpens?"

"You know what he's been doin' in there, don't you?" Deke asked. He laughed. "He's been tryin' to find hisself a date for the Saterday night dances. Some of them farmers' pigs is prettier'n some of their daughters."

Slim laughed. "Now that's a fact. That's truly a fact. Onliest thing is, Flannigan, when you do that, you got to wipe your feet off when you come out. Most especial, iffen you are plannin' on comin' into a place where they's men tryin' to drink."

Pat drained the rest of his whiskey, left a coin on the bar, and started to leave. He had no intention of becoming embroiled in an altercation with a couple of drunken cowboys.

"Hey, you ain't leavin', are you?" Deke asked.

"Yeah, he's leavin'," Slim said. "Didn't you read in the paper this week? Mr. Flannigan don't like to make no comments. Ain't that right, Flannigan? You don't like to make no comments?"

Pat tried to walk by them, but both of them stepped away from the bar and took up a position to block his exit.

"Now, you don't want to leave without makin' some kind of comment, do you?" Deke asked. He grinned broadly.

"Yeah," Slim said. "Tell us what you think about the big trail drive, why don't you?"

"Don't that seem a little strange to you, Flannigan?" Deke asked. "What do you think about the ranchers drivin' their cows to Boise, when they could send 'em on your train?"

"It's the cattlemen's business," Pat said. "They can do what they wish with their own cows."

"Well, now, what do you think of that? He *can* talk," Slim said.

"If you gentlemen will excuse me, I'll be on my way," Pat said.

"Naw," Deke said. He smiled broadly, showing a mouthful of crooked, broken teeth. "Naw, we ain't gonna excuse you. We're gonna keep you aroun', and maybe have a little fun with you."

"If you keep me around, gentlemen, I assure you, you won't have any fun," Pat said.

"Oh, I think we will," Deke said, and he took a swing at Pat.

Pat had been braced for it because he saw Deke tensing long before he actually swung. He was able to avoid Deke's wild swing easily. The swing left Deke off balance, and Pat counter-punched with a short, powerful blow, right into Deke's solar plexus.

Deke went down, gasping for breath, and Pat turned his attention to Slim, who was so surprised by the sudden turn of events that he hadn't even raised his fist. Pat drew his arm back to hit him.

"No, Flannigan, no!" Slim said, raising his hands. "It was Deke that started the fight, not me."

Pat looked at Slim, cowering before him, and he let out a snort of disgust.

"Take care of your friend before he pukes on the floor," Pat said, walking out of the saloon.

CHAPTER TWENTY

Mattie left the house with the first gray light of morning. The sun, still low in the east, sent long bars of light slashing through the trees, and the morning mist curled around the tops of the trees like wisps of smoke. She could feel the excitement of a cattle drive, before she could hear the sounds, and she could hear the crying and bawling of cattle, and the shouts and whistles of the wranglers, before she could actually see the herd.

More than twenty-five hundred head of cattle milled about on the high plateau of the Buckthorn Ranch. They represented the combined herds of half a dozen ranchers, all of whom had come together for the trail drive to Boise. When Mattie crested the last ridge, she could see them. They were in a natural pen, bordered on the south by a sheer drop to the Owyhee River, and on the east by the narrow draw from which the river emerged. Cowboys darted about on the north and west flanks, whistling, and keeping the herd in check.

Mattie knew that this was the most critical time for the herd, for the cows had been thrown together and they were aware of different smells and feelings, and they would be nervous. The least thing could spook them, so the cowboys had to be very careful.

The chuck wagon was parked to one side of the herd, so Mattie rode toward it, keeping along the edge of the precipice so as not to spook the herd. She wanted to go down to the wagon to speak with the cook.

Mattie was familiar with chuck wagons, because her first round-up, as a little girl, had been as a cook's helper, and she had been fascinated by the honeycombs and cubbyholes of the chuck box. The chuck box sat at the rear of the wagon, with a hinged lid which let down onto a swinging leg to form a worktable. Here the cook stored his utensils and whatever food he might use during the day; such things as flour, sugar, dried fruit, coffee beans, pinto beans, tobacco, "medicinal" whiskey, and, when Mattie was a little girl, hard candy.

"Well, hello, Miss Mattie," the cook said, as Mattie got off her horse and helped herself to a cup of coffee from the pot which hung, percolating, over the fire. "Are you going on the trail drive with us?"

"No, John," Mattie said brightly. "I wish I could go. I remember when I was a little girl."

John laughed. "Yes, you thought the possibles drawer was made just for a little girl's candy, didn't you?"

"I sure did," Mattie said. "I guess those days are over now. I'm not a little girl anymore."

"No, ma'am, I guess you're not," John said, and as he looked at her, Mattie suddenly got the feeling that he was thinking of the stories which were circulating about her. Then he grew embarrassed, and coughed, and looked down.

"John, have you seen James this morning?" Mattie asked.

"Yes, ma'am, I seen 'im," John said. "Fact is, he said if anybody was lookin' for 'im, to have 'em wait, 'cause he was gonna come right back here after he rode around the herd to check on things."

"All right, fine, I'll wait here," Mattie said.

Mattie had just finished her coffee when James rode up. She tossed the last dregs out and smiled at him.

"How's your shoulder holding out?" she asked. "Any problem with riding?"

"Not a bit," James said. He moved his arm around, demonstrating the mobility which had returned. "Thanks to some good nursing, recovery was complete."

* * *

"How long do we have 'afore one of these things goes off, once we light 'em?" a tall, rawboned young man asked Peter Wemmer.

Peter pointed to the fuse on the end of the stick of dynamite the man was holding.

"If you light it out on the end like you're supposed to, you'll have about seven seconds."

"Seven seconds? Is that all? That ain't very long when you're a' holdin' onto a stick of dynamite," one of the others said.

"Listen," Peter said angrily. "Do you want to get even with those bastards for killin' Lars, or don't you?"

"Well, yes, of course we do," another answered.

"Then don't be such a yellow-belly, and listen to me," Peter said.

Peter was talking to half a dozen young men, all between the ages of sixteen and twenty. They were sons of settlers, and they felt the animosity of the ranchers and the community very keenly. They also felt a strong awareness of Lars's untimely death, and it was to avenge that death that they had gathered here, in the same draw where Lars had been killed.

"Are we gonna try and kill the cattle with dynamite?"

"No," Peter said. "Some cattle may be killed, but if so, why then that's just a part of it 'n' it can't be helped."

"Go over the plan one more time."

Peter sighed. "All right but pay attention this time. Now, out there, all the ranchers who are goin' to drive their cows back to Boise have got 'em put together in one herd."

"They sure is a bunch of 'em," someone said, looking out from the draw over the high plateau where the cattle had congregated.

"There are more than two thousand," Peter said. "I know that for a fact."

"Whew," someone whistled, "that's a lot of beef eatin'."

The others laughed, but Peter regained their attention. He held up a few sticks of dynamite.

"These here sticks of dynamite are our weapons. We light one, throw it, light another, throw it, then light another and throw it. We got to do it all in six seconds, see, because the first one is going to go off in seven seconds, and we've got to be out of there."

"Are we each going to have three?"

"No," Peter said. "I could only come up with fifteen sticks, so some will have two. You won't have any problem. It's them with three that'll have a problem. But now look at the fuse. You have to make sure you light it here, out on the end, for it has to have that long to burn for seven seconds. Iffen you light it here, or here," he touched the middle of the fuse, and then the part of the fuse nearest the stick itself, "it'll go off pretty fast."

"Boom!" one of the young men shouted, and the others

laughed nervously.

"Now, this here ain't no laughin' matter," Peter said seriously.

"Come on, Peter, you're a' soundin' like a cap'n in the army. We ain't no army."

"Yes," Peter said seriously. "Yes, we are an army. Don't you see? We got us a real, live war goin' on here. It's us agin' the ranchers, 'n' iffen we don' win, they are gonna run us right off this land 'n' back to Ohio or Missouri or wherever we all come from. We got to fight to keep a' holt of what's rightly ours."

"Peter's right," one of the others said. "We got us a real war goin' on here."

"Wow, then Peter *is* like a cap'n, ain't he?"

"Yes," Peter said. "And when your cap'n talks, the rest of you got to pay attention."

"We know what we got to do," one of the others said. "Let's jes' git on our horses 'n' go on down there and do it."

"All right," Peter said. "Let's do it. Remember, throw them as far as you can, light another an' then throw it. But don't throw 'em at each other. Throw 'em out in the herd."

Peter and the other young men mounted their horses, though in two cases, the mounts weren't horses but mules, and rode out toward the herd.

Suddenly there were a series of stomach-jarring explosions, one right after another. The herd of cattle, nervous anyway, reacted immediately. Twenty-five hundred animals started a mad, panic-stricken stampede, heading straight for Mattie.

Mattie had been so startled by the explosions that for an instant she forgot about the herd. Then, when she perceived her danger, it was too late. The herd was thundering toward her, and she had nowhere to go but the sheer drop of more than two hundred feet. She did the only thing she could do, and that was to try to ride right through the thundering stampede, hoping the cows would open a path for her.

Mattie might have made it, had she been astride a pony which was trained to work cattle. But this morning she had chosen to ride a horse that had been bred for speed, rather than work, and the horse was terrified of the onrushing cows. He wanted to depend on his one, proven commodity, speed, to get him out of the danger, because he didn't know of the drop-off behind him. As a result, instead of a finely coordinated effort of horse and rider to escape the danger, it became a battle between them. The horse tried to obey its own instincts and failed to respond to Mattie's directions. It fell in the middle of the herd, and Mattie was thrown beneath the flashing hooves.

Mattie's last conscious thought was of Nora. Who would warn her about James now?

CHAPTER TWENTY-ONE

For the third time in as many weeks, the cemetery was the scene of an emotional funeral. This time it was for Mattie Andrews, and the mourners bewailed not only her death, but the senseless slaughter of more than four hundred cattle, also killed in the stampede.

Mattie had always been a popular figure in the valley, and no one who attended the funeral could look at her coffin without thinking of the vivacious young girl whose brilliant ride had won the Fourth of July race just a short time before. Forgotten now was the fact that she had so recently been the object of their scorn, and women who had snubbed her just a few days before now wept openly and unashamedly.

Pat attended the funeral, even though he realized that his presence would be unwelcome. He didn't care what they thought. He had come for Mattie.

No one spoke to Pat during the service.

Several glared at him with ill-concealed hostility, and Nora avoided his glance every time he looked in her direction.

After the funeral, Pat walked up to Buck Andrews to

extend his condolences.

"Why are you here?" Buck asked Pat.

"I am here to pay my respects to your daughter, Mr. Andrews," Pat said. "I thought she was a wonderful young woman."

"You speak of respect?" Buck replied. "How can you speak of respect? The entire valley knows how you treat respect. You ruined my little Mattie's reputation."

"Mr. Andrews, I'm sorry you feel that way," Pat said.

"How do you expect me to feel?" Buck replied angrily.

Nora saw the two men speaking and she came over to speak to them.

"Mr. Andrews, if there is anything any of us can do," Nora said.

"Anything at all," James added. James was right behind Nora. "You just ask us."

"There is nothing anyone can do," Buck said. "Nothing."

Nora looked around the cemetery with a confused look on her face. "James, where are Sweeney and the other cowboys?"

"What?" James answered.

"Sweeney, Deke, Slim, and the others. Surely, they would come to Mattie's funeral. They thought so much of her."

"I guess they just had something else to do," James said noncommittally.

"Something else to do?" Pat asked. "Wilson, what are you saying?"

"I'm saying that the men had something else to do today, and they couldn't make it to Mattie's funeral."

"Mr. Andrews, do *you* know what Wilson is talking about?" Pat asked Buck.

"No," Buck said, "but it must be important for them

to be absent."

"James, what is it?" Nora asked. "Where are they?"

James sighed. "Well, you might as well know," he said. "Slim recognized one of the riders who stampeded the cattle as Peter Wemmer. So Sweeney took some men out to Wemmer's cabin. They are going to bring him in."

"Bring him in?" Pat asked. "Bring him in, or lynch him? Wilson, if anything happens to Wemmer, his blood will be on your hands."

"No, Flannigan, his blood will be on *your* hands," Buck said. "As is the blood of everyone else who has died in this range war."

"There will be no range war," Pat said. "Not if everyone keeps their heads. Mr. Andrews, the ranchers respect you. Talk to them, urge them to remain calm."

"And who will urge the farmers to remain calm?" Buck asked.

"You can," Nora said to Pat. "The farmers will listen to you."

"Not if the Wemmer boy is lynched," Pat said.

"James, go out there," Nora said. "Go out and see that nothing happens."

"I'll go with you," Pat said. "Maybe we can stop this thing before it goes any further."

"There's only one way to really stop it," James said. "You started it, when you opened up a peaceful valley to immigrants, outsiders who have no respect for the rights or property of others, people who have no appreciation for what we have built here. Now the only way we can have peace is for you to stop selling land to the immigrants."

"That has nothing to do with whether or not Wemmer is lynched by that mob you sent out there," Pat said. "Now, are you going to go out there and stop them, or not?"

"Please go, James," Nora urged.

"All right," James said. "I'll go out there, Flannigan. But I can't promise you that I'll be able to do anything. The men were pretty riled up about Mattie's murder."

Slim Tucker drained the last of his bottle and threw it against the rocks. The bottle smashed with a tinkling crash, and the pieces of glass flashed in the noonday sun as they scattered across the ground. He scratched his crotch and belched as he stared across the open space toward the small log cabin.

"Well, what the hell?" Slim said. He belched again.

"What are you getting so antsy about?" Deke asked. "Sit down and take it easy. He has to come out sometime."

"I don't want to wait for the son-of-a-bitch to come out. I wanna kill the bastard now."

"We're gonna kill 'im," Sweeney said. "I'm just tryin' to figure on the best way to do it, that's all."

"Wait a minute," Deke said. "Sweeney, you said we was gonna take 'im in to the sheriff. You didn't say nothin' 'bout killin' 'im."

"Sure, we're gonna take 'im in," Sweeney said. "If he'll go peaceful. But if he ain't willin' to go peaceful, then we're gonna take 'im in anyway. And it don't much seem like he wants to go in peaceful, now, does it?"

"I don't intend to be any party to a lynchin'," Deke said.

"It's too bad we don't have no dynamite," Sweeney mused. "Iffen we had us a little dynamite we could blast 'im outta there."

"Hell, I don' need no dynamite," Slim said. "He's jus' a damn pig-farmer. I can get 'im outta there by myself."

"Yeah? And just how do you intend to do that?" Sweeney asked.

"Watch." Slim said. Slim pulled his pistol and started running toward the log cabin, blazing away.

"Slim!" Deke shouted. "Slim, come back here, you damn fool!"

Slim ran all the way to the front porch, firing his six-shooter at the house. There was no answering fire, and when Slim reached the front porch, he turned around and shouted back to the others who were holed up in the rocks.

"See! I told you there was nothin' to it! Now come on, let's pull this chicken liver outta here and hang 'im!"

At that moment, the front door of the cabin opened, and Peter Wemmer stepped out, holding a shotgun levelled toward Slim.

"Slim, look out!" Deke called.

At Deke's warning shout, Slim turned back toward the door. The smile of triumph on his face changed to a look of surprise, then fear, as the shotgun roared.

Slim's chest and stomach turned red as the load of buckshot exposed his insides. The charge of the shotgun knocked Slim back against the supporting post of the porch roof, and the impact tore the post away, bringing the roof crashing down. Slim fell back onto the ground, writhing in agony.

"Slim!" Deke called, and he stood up to go after his friend, but Sweeney grabbed him and pulled him back down.

"You want to wind up the same way?" he asked. "Get down, get out of his line of fire."

"But Slim's out there!"

Deke watched in horror as Slim kicked and twitched a few times, then lay still.

"Damn you!" Deke called, and his voice returned in an angry, accusing echo. Everyone thought Deke was

188 | ROBERT VAUGHAN

swearing at Wemmer, but he added, "Damn you, Slim! You fool! What did you do that for?"

"Andy," Sweeney called to one of the other men, "did you bring the kerosene?"

"Yeah," Andy said, "I brought it."

"I was gonna burn a couple of fields," Sweeney said. "But I got me a better idea."

"What you want me to do with it?"

"You think you can get down there and splash it on the side of the house?" Sweeney asked. "Me 'n the other boys could start firin', 'n that way Wemmer'd have to keep his head down."

"Yeah," Andy said, "I can do it."

"We'll burn the bastard out," Sweeney said. Andy took the kerosene and a box of matches, then started toward the cabin, running in a bent-over position, keeping low, behind a ridge line.

"When he gets there, start firin' at the front of the house," Sweeney told the others. "But be careful you don't hit Andy."

A moment later Andy popped up behind the ridge, and when he did, Sweeney gave the signal to the others to open fire.

Nearly a dozen guns began firing, and the sound of the gun shots rolled back from the walls of the nearby canyon like thunder. It had the desired effect, and Peter Wemmer kept his head down, so he didn't see Andy splash kerosene onto the side of the cabin and strike a match. When Andy ran back to the ridge, the entire side of the cabin was enveloped in flame.

"Now," Sweeney said, after the firing ceased. "All we have to do is wait. He'll be out in a minute and we'll have him."

"Give him a chance to surrender," Deke said.

"Slim was your friend, not mine," Sweeney said. "I figured you'd want the first shot."

"I want to do it legal," Deke said.

The cowboys held their guns anxiously and looked at the cabin, watching for any sign of Peter Wemmer. The flames climbed the wall and leaped to the roof of the cabin. The shake shingles caught fire quickly, and the fire soon spread to the front wall, and then to the other side, so that the entire cabin was one roaring inferno. Flames and smoke boiled high into the sky, but still Peter Wemmer did not appear. "Where is he?" the cowboys asked.

"How can he stay in there?"

"Why don't he come out?"

The flames roared and cracked, and even from their vantage point, the cowboys were driven back by the heat.

Still, Peter Wemmer did not appear.

"Hey, Sweeney, they's a couple of riders comin'," one of the cowboys called.

Sweeney stood up and looked at the approaching riders.

"One of 'em is Mr. Wilson," Sweeney said. "I can tell by the way he's sittin' his horse."

"Who's the other fella?"

"It's Flannigan," someone else said.

"Flannigan? What's he doin' here?"

"I reckon we're about to find out," Sweeney said matter-of-factly.

Pat and James dismounted when they reached the group of men, and Pat looked toward the burning cabin.

"What's that?" he asked. "What's going on here?"

"That's Wemmer's cabin," Sweeney said. "We set it afire to try 'n get him to come out."

"Try?" Pat said, looking at Sweeney quickly. "What do

you mean, try?"

"Just what I said, mister, try," Sweeney said. "He didn't come out."

"You mean he's still in there?"

"Yep."

"Damnit, Wilson, your men burned him *alive,*" Pat swore angrily.

"We didn't intend to burn him," Sweeney said. "We was jus' tryin' to get him to come out. He stayed in there of his own accord."

"Besides, the son-of-a-bitch kilt Slim," one of the other cowboys said.

"To say nothin' of killin' Miss Mattie," Sweeney added. "If you want my way of thinkin', he got his just reward."

Pat walked toward the blazing cabin, but he couldn't get too far before he hit a blistering wall of heat. He stood there, watching as the house began to fall in on itself, and he felt sick at heart. Maybe James was right. Maybe he was responsible for all of this.

"Get them out of here, Wilson," Pat said quietly.

"You men go on back to the ranch," James said.

"If you don't mind, Mr. Wilson," Deke said. "I'd like to stay till I can get Slim's body back."

"That might not be such a good idea," James said. "The squatters are sure to see the smoke. When they do, they'll come over here, and if they find you, it wouldn't go good for you. You'd better come with us."

"I'm not leavin' Slim's body here for the vultures," Deke said. "And that means the critters who walk on two legs as well as the critters that fly."

"I'll stay," Pat offered. "I'll get his body for you."

"You'll stay?" Deke asked. "What for? I don't see you as carin' much about Slim, one way or the other."

"I didn't want to see him killed," Pat said. "Nor did I want to see Peter, or Mattie, or Lars, or the professor killed. And I especially don't want to see anyone else killed. I'll stay."

"Why, I...I appreciate that, Flannigan," Deke said.

"Will you be able to handle the squatters if they come?" James asked.

"I don't know," Pat said. "Maybe I can convince them that Slim and Martin killed each other. If it'll stop the range war, it'll be worth the try."

"There's only one way to really stop it," James said. "And I told you what that was."

"I know," Pat replied. He paused for a moment, then drew a deep breath. "That's why I'm not going to sell any more of the range land. I'm stopping the immigration."

"Are you serious?" James asked.

"Yes," Pat said quietly. "Call it a wedding present for you and Nora if you like. You won, Wilson."

CHAPTER TWENTY-TWO

Headlines in the *Valley Monitor:*

RANGE WAR ENDS!
Peace Comes to the Valley

Unsold Range Land to be used for grazing
After a terrible series of killings,
violence and wanton destruction, the
range war which has set farmer against
rancher and neighbor against neighbor
has come to an end. It was ended when Pat
Flannigan, President of the Valley Spur
Railroad, and James Wilson, President of
the Valley River Cattlemen's Association,
reached a compromise.

James Wilson has stated that the ranch-
ers will honor the claims of those immi-
grants who are already settled, and Pat
Flannigan has agreed to sell no more land.
This newspaper commends both gentlemen
for their diplomacy and prays that the peace
thus effected shall be a lasting one.

When the newspapers were fresh off the press and still smelled of the ink, Nora took one copy over to the depot to give to Pat. As the paper contained her wedding announcement, she thought it would be better if she gave it to Pat in person.

The depot was much quieter than it had been in the past. Whereas it had been fairly bustling with the arrival of new immigrants and their belongings, the cessation of selling the land had brought a halt to the railroad business. Now the depot was empty, and only two boxes of freight sat on the loading platform. Nora didn't know whether it was freight which had already arrived and was awaiting claim, or freight which was to be shipped out. The fact that there were only two boxes somehow made the depot look less busy than if there were no boxes at all.

Ira was inside, but Pat wasn't around. Nora stood on the depot floor, holding the copy of the paper she was going to give Pat, and looked around. She saw the clock, the same one she had seen put on the wall on the day she had helped clean up the place for the meeting Pat had conducted to announce the introduction of rail service to the valley. That seemed like so long ago, though in reality it was but two months past.

"Hello, Miss Cassidy," Ira said. "Is there anything I can do for you?"

"Is Mr. Flannigan around?" Nora asked.

"Yes, ma'am," Ira said. "He's out workin' on the engine."

"Oh? Is there something wrong with it?" Nora asked anxiously.

"Nothing bad," Ira said. "A few adjustments that have to be made. Now that we aren't so busy, we'll be able to get it back in shape. Not that it matters any," he added.

"What do you mean, not that it matters?" Nora asked.

"Simple," Ira said. "With no immigrant travel, we have no business. And there haven't been enough immigrants moving in to provide steady business, so we'll go under."

"But no, must you?" Nora asked. "The railroad could mean so much to the valley."

"All it's meant so far is trouble," Ira said. "If you ask me, I wish there was some way we could take up the track 'n lay it somewhere else. It's not like that printin' press Pat bought for you. You can go anywhere with it. We're stuck here."

"What?" Nora asked, shocked by Ira's offhand comment. "What did you just say?"

"I said we're stuck here." '

"No, I mean about the printing press. Did you say that *Mr. Flannigan* bought it?"

"Yes, ma'am," Ira said. "He got it from a fella up in Bakertown."

"Are you sure?"

"I can show you the invoice if you want, Miss Cassidy," Ira said.

"No, that's quite all right," Nora replied.

"I thought you knew."

"No, I had no idea."

Ira chuckled. "Well, if you know Pat Flannigan like I know 'im, you wouldn't be none surprised by that. He's always doin' one good turn or another without takin' any of the credit for it. Why, you take these here immigrants, now. He's done loaned money to more'n half of 'em, 'n' believe me, Miss Cassidy, he don' have any money to loan. It's jus' that he does things like that 'cause he's a man with a heart that's good as gold."

"Where is the engine?"

Ira smiled. "Well now, you can't miss it," he said. "All you gotta do is follow the track. It's down to the west end of the terminal."

"Thanks," Nora said.

She left the depot and walked along the tracks toward the engine. It was sitting, naked and alone, at the end of the track, next to the bumper. There were no cars attached to it, and it looked much as it had on the day she had ridden in the engine cab with Pat.

Nora heard a clanking sound as she approached, and when she got there, she saw a pair of legs protruding from beneath the engine, from between the two large driver wheels.

"Emmett, is that you?" a voice asked. Nora recognized the voice as Pat's. "Hand me the spanner wrench, will you?"

There was an open toolbox on the ground, and Nora looked inside. She had no idea which wrench was a spanner, but she picked up the first tool her hand touched and passed it beneath the engine to him.

"No," Pat said. "The spanner wrench."

"I don't know what a spanner wrench is," Nora said.

"Nora! Is that you?" Pat said, and as he started out from under the engine, he bumped his head. "Ouch!"

"Are you all right?"

"Yes," Pat said, rubbing his head gingerly. He sat up and smiled at Nora. "What brings you here?"

"I thought I would deliver you a copy of the paper," Nora said.

"Well now," Pat replied, smiling broadly. "Now that's what I call service. It isn't everyone who gets the paper personally delivered by the publisher, is it?"

"No," Nora said. "But then, everyone didn't buy the equipment for me. You did."

"How did you find out?" Pat asked. "I told Post that it was to be kept a secret."

"Mr. Post didn't tell me," Nora said.

"Who did?"

"Never mind," Nora replied. "You did buy the equipment, didn't you? I'm in business because of you."

"You are in business because the *Valley Monitor* is a good newspaper."

"Do you really think so?"

"Of course, I do. If I didn't, I wouldn't say so."

"There have been articles printed in the paper which upset you," Nora said.

"Yes."

"And yet you were willing to put the paper back in business. Don't you think that looks a little suspicious?"

"What do you mean?"

"Maybe you were trying to ease your conscience for having destroyed the paper in the first place."

"I didn't destroy it, Nora."

"Yes, I know, we all know. You were with Mattie."

Pat stood and cross one arm across his chest, held his elbow with that hand, bowed his head for a moment as he pinched his nose.

"No," he finally said. "I wasn't with Mattie that night."

"What? But that was the alibi that got you out of jail."

"Yes."

"Why did Mattie say that, if you weren't with her?"

"She knew I didn't do it."

"How did she know?"

"She said it was because she knew who *did* do it."

"Who did do it?"

"She never told me."

"I...Pat...I don't know what to say."

"That's all right. At this point, too much has been said already."

James and his foreman were riding along the shores of the Owyhee River. The river trailed out behind the riders, cascading in wild, rushing white water, tumbling, and roaring its way down to the valley floor, behind and below them. From up here the entire valley was visible: the town a neat collection of houses and stores, the ranches, large even from this perspective, and the farms neat and orderly, with the fields of crops making checkerboard squares.

"There," Sweeney said, pointing to a rock overhang. "That's what I was talkin' about. Iffen a body was to bring that thing down into the river channel, why the water'd have to flow through the old Green River bed."

"There is no riverbed for the Green River anymore," James said. "The water only went there during flood stage, and since the dam, there's no way for it to get through."

"But iffen the dam was to be broke at about the same time them rocks was dropped in the diversion channel, what then?" Sweeney asked.

James studied the Owyhee, and the diversion channel for a while, then twisted in his saddle and looked down toward the valley. The Green River bed used to run right through the part of the valley which was now occupied by the farmers. He grinned.

"It would cut a new riverbed," he said.

"Right smack dab through the center of ever' pig farmer in the valley," Sweeney said.

"With their crops flooded, they'd have no reason to stay," James said. "How soon can you get it done?"

CHAPTER TWENTY-THREE

The main house at Buckthorn Ranch might have been the most popular night club in San Francisco, for all its laughter and gaiety. James was throwing a party to celebrate his wedding to Nora, and there were guests from all over the state. Nearly every resident of town and nearly every rancher was there. Only the farmers were conspicuous by their absence.

The party began at one o'clock in the afternoon and was to continue until four, at which time the marriage ceremony would be performed. It was now nearly four, and the party had been going on all afternoon. There were more people than the house could accommodate, so many of the guests moved out onto the lawn, where they continued to celebrate.

Music spilled out from the house, played not by one of the bands which ordinarily performed for the Saturday night dances, but by a full orchestra, hired by James just for the occasion.

Tables were piled with glazed hams, roast duck and chicken, and fruits and vegetables of every color and texture. On the lawn two steer halves were spitted, and they turned slowly over open fires.

Liquid refreshment shared honors with all the food, for there were several bars established, one in the parlor, one in the dining room, and one in the main hall. If anyone had a thirst, no matter where they were, they were but a moment away from satisfying their need.

"Hey, James!" one of the ranchers called. "I just saw the parson arrive. This business is getting serious!"

The rancher's comment was greeted with laughter, and Father Crawford pinkened with embarrassment when he walked into the middle of such a celebration.

"Are you all ready, vicar?" James asked.

Father Crawford pulled at his collar with his finger and looked around the house, as the party continued in full force, totally unaware of his presence.

"Yes," he said. "I can't help but feel, however, that the marriage vows would have been better served in church."

"Surely the Lord wouldn't mind a man celebrating his wedding in his own house?" James challenged.

"The celebration is in order," Father Crawford said. "But the sacrament of marriage should not turn into a——a drunken revelry."

"I'll get them quiet before the wedding," James said. "You can count on that."

"Where is Nora?" Father Crawford asked.

"She's in the guest room, getting ready for the ceremony," James said, pointing upstairs. "I haven't seen her since she arrived, early this morning."

"I'll have a few words with her, if you don't mind."

"Have all the words you want, parson," James said. "But tell her that it's nearly time. We must be married by four."

Father Crawford chuckled. "Oh, surely there's no

precise timetable."

"Yes, there is," James said. "I have an announcement to make at exactly four o'clock, and then I want to be married."

"Very well, I shall tell her."

Nora sat at the dresser, critically examining the reflection that stared back at her. Not one hair was out of place. Her brown eyes were cool and appraising, her complexion smooth. And yet, there was something wrong.

"I'm just nervous," she said to herself. "I once heard that all brides are nervous, just before they are married."

Nora got up from the dresser and walked over to the window. She looked out at the partygoers who were celebrating on the lawn below her. Then she looked back toward town. She could make out the church steeple and the roof of the hotel. But she couldn't quite see the depot. It was just beyond the hotel. Perhaps if she stood on a chair, she could see the roofline. Suddenly Nora blushed. What was she doing? She was trying to see the depot because her mind was on Pat Flannigan. But how could that be? She was about to be married. Surely, she wouldn't think of another man on her wedding day! And yet, she had only to close her eyes, and she could see him.

A knock on the door interrupted Nora's musings and startled her back to reality. The palms of her hands were sweating, and her skin was flushed. There was another knock. "Nora, it's me, Father Crawford."

"You can come in," Nora said.

Crawford stepped into the room, and as he looked at Nora in her wedding gown, he smiled.

"My, my, my," he said. "Never have I performed a ceremony for a more beautiful bride."

"Thank you," Nora said.

"It is such a shame that your father can't be here to see you like this. He would have been so proud."

"My father thought a great deal of James," Nora said. "I hope he is happy about this...that is, if a spirit can be happy."

"Of course, a spirit can be happy, child," Father Crawford said. "After all, isn't that the hope of Christianity?"

"I suppose so," Nora said.

"What is it, Nora? You seem strangely pensive."

"Do I? I'm sorry, I guess it's just nervousness. Aren't all brides nervous?"

"Nervous, yes," Father Crawford said. "Pensive, no. Nora, are you absolutely certain that you want to do this?"

"Of course, I am," Nora said quickly. "What makes you think I'm not?"

"I don't know," Father Crawford said. "Maybe it's just a feeling I have."

"Anyway, it's too late to be having second thoughts now," Nora said. "I'm about to be married."

"No, it's not too late now," Father Crawford said. "After the ceremony, it will be too late."

There was another knock on the door, and Mrs. Oliver called out.

"Nora, honey, it's time. Is the parson in there?"

Father Crawford looked at Nora, and Nora took a deep breath, then nodded at him. "I'm ready," she said quietly.

"We're coming now," Father Crawford called back.

Nora waited for Father Crawford to go downstairs. Then she picked up her bouquet and went down the stairs. At the foot of the stairs she looked into the parlor. The parlor had been filled with chairs, though an aisle had been left in the middle to allow her to walk through to the front.

"There she is," someone whispered.

"Oh, isn't she lovely?" one of the women said quietly.

The orchestra began playing the *Wedding March*, and Nora moved gracefully down the center aisle toward Father Crawford and James. She moved into position to the right of James.

"Dearly beloved," Father Crawford began. "We have come together—"

Suddenly the house shook with the sound of distant explosions, and there was a buzz of curiosity among the people.

"Don't be alarmed," James said, turning toward them and holding his hands up be alarmed, that was just Sweeney." He smiled broadly. "He just blew the diversion channel dam."

"What?" Buck shouted. "What the hell did he want to do a crazy thing like that for?"

James pointed through the window toward the settlers' farms. "Just to take care of a little unfinished business," he said. "By tonight, every field these damned squatters have planted will be under water. They'll be ruined."

"James!" Nora said. "You did that?"

"Yes," James said proudly. "After tonight, this valley will be just like it was in the days before the immigrants arrived. They will all go home, believe me."

"Don't you understand?" Nora asked. "This *is* their home."

James laughed weakly. "Honey, that's no way for a rancher's wife to act."

"You're right," Nora said. "It is no way for a rancher's wife to act. Thank God, I'm *not* a rancher's wife. Father Crawford, did you bring your buggy?"

"Yes, I did, child."

"How quickly can you get me into town?"

"I can have you there in under ten minutes," Father Crawford said, snapping the prayer book closed.

"You can't walk out on me!" James said as Nora started toward the door. "Do you hear me? You can't walk out on me!"

"Watch me!" Nora said, and, angrily, she tossed the bouquet back over her shoulder.

True to his word, Father Crawford had Nora in town in less than ten minutes. She directed him to the depot, and when the buggy stopped, she hopped out and ran inside with her veil and train streaming out behind her.

"Pat!" she called. "Pat, are you here?" Pat stepped out of his room and looked at Nora in total shock.

"My God, girl, what are you doin' here?" he asked.

"There's no time for all that now," she said. "Sweeney's blown the diversion channel dam. All the farmers are going to be flooded out!"

"What?"

"The Green riverbed runs through the land the farmers have been settling. That land is all going to be under water soon. We've got to warn them. They may be in danger."

"Damn!" Pat swore. "Ira, Ira, get out here!"

When Ira appeared, also shocked by Nora's appearance, Pat told him what Nora said. "Get Emmett," he said. "We've got to warn Forsberg and the others."

The sound of hoofbeats made them look outside, and Deke swung down from his horse, almost before the animal had stopped running. He came inside.

"You!" Pat said, stepping toward him. "Is this the way the cattlemen honor their agreements?"

"Now hold on, Flannigan," Deke said, holding up his hand. "I didn't have nothin' to do with this. Nothin' at all, 'n neither did Mr. Andrews, nor any of the other ranchers. It was all Wilson's doin'."

"Well, whoever's doin' it was, it's too late now," Pat said. "The damage is done. We've got to get the farmers out of there."

"We can save their crops," Deke said.

"What?" Pat asked.

"We can save their crops," Deke said again. "If we can get enough people 'n enough shovels, we can close in Indian Chute. That way the water can't get into the old riverbed."

"Yes!" Nora said excitedly. "Pat, that will work. Oh, but—it would take so many people."

"Well," Deke said, smiling broadly, "if Flannigan can get the pig farmers to pitch in, I guess there'll be enough. Look outside at what's comin'."

Pat and Nora walked over to the door and Nora gasped. There were more than forty men approaching the depot, all carrying shovels, axes, and handsaws. There were cowboys and ranchers, and even some of the clerks and merchants from the town. Most were still in their suits, having just come from the party.

"Deke, isn't Indian Chute close to where the damn was blown?" Pat asked.

"Yes, no more'n a quarter of a mile away."

"Emmett, make up the train," Pat said. "Ira, you round up the farmers. Tell them to get to the track and we'll pick 'em up. Come on, we'll take the train to Indian Chute!"

While Emmett and Ira went about their jobs, Pat went out front and told the gathering men what he had in mind. They let out a cheer and headed for the cars.

Emmett had the engine backed up and connected to the cars in a few moments. Pat climbed up into the engine cab, then reached down and helped Nora up behind him.

"Does it look familiar?" he asked her, smiling broadly.

"It looks wonderful," Nora said.

Emmett opened the throttle and the engine started, jerking the line of cars until the entire train was in motion. The steam puffed and roared, and the train began moving at a pretty good clip.

"Blow the whistle," Pat said to Nora, pointing toward the whistle cord. "We need to let the farmers know we're coming."

"I get to blow the whistle?"

"That you do, Miss Cassidy," Pat said. "Or is it Mrs. Wilson?"

"It is not Mrs. Wilson," Nora said resolutely. "And it never will be!" She punctuated her comment by pulling hard on the whistle cord, and the whistle called out to everyone that the train was in motion.

All along the track, farmers met the train, so that by the time it reached Indian Chute, it was full of people, farmers and their wives and children, ranchers, and their hands.

"All right," Pat called to them. "We've got to close in Indian Chute. If we can, that will force the water back into the lake, and it'll cut its way through to the McCauley channel."

The water had already begun to flow through the diversion channel by the time they started working, and they had to stand knee deep and shovel mud. They worked side by side, farmer, rancher, and merchant, digging in the mud, piling up a hasty dam. A couple of times they nearly had it stopped, only to see a large, mud wall collapse, and they had to start over again.

"Mr. Forsberg!" Deke suddenly shouted. "Mr. Forsberg, look out!"

Deke had seen a boulder loosened by the water start to tumble toward Forsberg, and only his timely shout prevented Forsberg from being seriously injured. Forsberg managed to jump aside just in time.

"Thank you, young man," Forsberg said gratefully, after the boulder crashed into the mud right where he had been standing.

"That's all right," Deke answered, embarrassed.

The others had seen the close call as well. Then Pat got an idea.

"Men, we're going about this all wrong," he said. "Let's get up there and loosen as many rocks as we can. If we can get them to fall into the chute, they'll hold better than the mud."

At Pat's suggestion the workers clambered up the side of the hill and began working. After about thirty minutes of labor, the rocks started to slide down. They fell slowly at first, then faster and faster until the chute was completely dammed up. There was a loud cheer of victory.

Pat looked over at Nora. She was still in her wedding dress, and it was black with mud. She saw him looking at her, then she looked down at herself and moaned.

"Oh," she said. "Oh, I look awful."

Pat smiled. "No, you don't," he said. "You look beautiful. In fact, I've never seen you look more beautiful."

"Pat," Emmett said. "I think someone should go over to the diversion channel and blow the dam that Sweeney put across the river channel."

"That's a good idea," Pat said. "Would you do it?"

"I'll go with you," Deke offered. "Oh, by the way, before I go, I've got to get a couple of things off my chest. I think everybody should know that cow they said come from Boise was one of our own with a doctored brand. It didn't have no hoof 'n mouth disease—James put sulphuric acid on its hooves so it would look like it was infected. And Miss Cassidy..." Deke put his head down. "This is hard to say but it was Sweeny what blowed up the newspaper office. James told him to do it, 'n he planned to blame it on Flannigan. But to be honest, there didn't James nor Sweeny neither one have no idea that your pa would be in there."

"Thank you, Sweeny," Sheriff Ferrell said. "When we get this flooding taken care of, I'll be calling on Mr. Sweeny and Mr. Wilson."

"Pat, I'll be going with these fellers over to the diversion channel," Emmett said. "But who will help you drive the engine? You've got to get these people back to town."

Pat looked over at Nora. "I've got someone in mind," he said. "Someone with experience, if she'll take the job."

"I'll take the job," Nora said.

Pat walked over to her and took her hands in his. "I ought to warn you," he said. "This is a job with a lifetime commitment. Will you still take it?"

"I'll take it," Nora replied.

"Well?" Ira shouted. "Are you just going to stand there, or are you going to kiss her?"

"I'm going to kiss her," Pat said, and he pulled her to him, pressing his lips against hers. The crowd cheered in lusty approval—but Nora heard only the pounding of her own heart.

A LOOK AT: THE CROCKETTS': WESTERN SAGA ONE

SADDLE UP FOR A NON-STOP RIDE IN VOLUME ONE OF A NEW WESTERN SAGA – FROM THE MAN WHO BROUGHT YOU THE CHANEY BROTHERS WESTERN SERIES.

During the Civil War, they sought justice outside of the law, paying back every Yankee raid with one of their own. No man could stop them… no woman could resist them… and no Yankee stood a chance when Will and Gid Crockett rode into town.

After their parents are murdered by a band of marauding Yankees, Will and Gid Crockett join William Quantrill and his gang of bloodthirsty raiders to seek revenge on the attackers.

Someone's about to mess with the Crocketts', and that means someone's about to be messed with back. Will and Gid don't like getting shot at, especially by varmints who don't have skill enough to kill them.

The Crocketts': Western Saga 1 includes: Trail of Vengeance, Slaughter in Texas, Law of the Rope and The Town That Wouldn't Die.

AVAILABLE NOW ON KINDLE

AUTHOR THE AUTHOR

Robert Vaughan sold his first book when he was 19. That was 57 years and nearly 500 books ago. He wrote the novelization for the mini series Andersonville. Vaughan wrote, produced, and appeared in the History Channel documentary Vietnam Homecoming.

His books have hit the NYT bestseller list seven times. He has won the Spur Award, the PORGIE Award (Best Paperback Original), the Western Fictioneers Lifetime Achievement Award, received the Readwest President's Award for Excellence in Western Fiction, is a member of the American Writers Hall of Fame and is a Pulitzer Prize nominee.

Manufactured by Amazon.ca
Acheson, AB

13112035R00127